RUTHLESS SMILE

THE DAMNED CREW #2

TATUM RAYNE

Ruthless Smile
The Damned Crew #2
Copyright © 2023 Tatum Rayne

Published by Hudson Indie Ink
www.hudsonindieink.com

This book is licensed for your personal enjoyment only.
This book may not be re-sold or given away to other people. If you would like to share this book with another person, please purchase an additional copy for each recipient. If you're reading this book and did not purchase it, or it wasn't purchased for your use only, then please return to your favourite book retailer and purchase your own copy. Thank you for respecting the hard work of this author.
All rights reserved.

This is a work of fiction. Names, characters, places, brands, media, and incidents are either the product of the authors imagination or are used fictitiously. The author acknowledges the trademark status and trademark owners of various products referred to in this work of fiction, which have been used without permission. The publication/use of these trademarks is not authorised, associated with, or sponsored by the trademark owners.

Ruthless Smile/Tatum Rayne

*This is for everyone who was told to wait for their Prince Charming,
but they prefer the broken Bad-Boys instead.*

1

MARCUS

"*Boys, meet Ryan.*" Hellion's words rattle around my head as I glower at the woman in front of me, she doesn't seem phased by anything... Not even the look on my face saying I want to murder her ass where she stands. Nope, instead, she's standing there with a big ass grin on her face. Has she not looked around? Hasn't she realized she's in a place full of people who wouldn't think twice about killing her with one command from Hellion? I feel my brothers stiffen at the side of me, a demonic sound rumbling in Kane's chest.

My head whips around to look at him as the noise continues, it's at odds with how he's been since Diamond came along. I thought he had finally become a sensible being, but that noise tells me that the brother I know is still well and truly under the shell of the father figure.

Hellion, the little tease, looks over her shoulder. Our eyes connect and she winks, a smirk tipping the edge of her lips.

"What're you doing here?" Hellion's voice is strong as she watches the newcomer, her body language is relaxed which only adds to my confusion. I step forward to back her up as she steps down off the porch, bringing herself closer to the cocky bitch.

Ryan lifts a single shoulder in a shrug, then turns her attention to her fingernails. She's using one of them to pick under her nails like she has all the fucking time in the world. What the fuck is going on? Who the fuck is this bitch not to be bothered by Hellion's presence, I cock my head, either this girl is more than we know, or she's got a death wish.

"Oi! You ignorant twat, Hellion spoke to you!" I growl, moving forward again, which brings me to the middle step of the porch.

Her eyes meet mine and a feral look takes over her features, she's looking at me like I'm nothing, her mouth is pinched. One brow lifted, like she could lose her shit any second but I can tell all this is a front from whatever is playing in her mind, but she doesn't show it as her gaze slowly working up and down the length of me.

"So?" she sasses, her eyes taking in her fill of me. "Now where the fuck have you three been all my life?"

"Ho—"

"It's fine, Cheshire," Hellion interrupts me, snapping out her words snap like the crack of a whip, stopping my insults before they can fly like poison darts.

"Like fuck, Hellion," I growl, taking another step down so I'm only one away from the ground. "Who the fuck is this bitch?!"

"Who the fuck are you talking to, Fido?" Ryan steps closer, and my body tenses as she whips two knives out of nowhere, her eyes gleaming like death itself. A massive, evil smile is on her face, showing too many teeth as the savage look takes over her features.

My eyes stay locked on hers, the challenge clear on her face. I launch off the step, my strides eating up the ground as she stands there. Yells fill the air and as I get closer, Hellion steps in my way. My eyes drop to hers as she glares at me. I growl at her, pissed that she blocked me from the disrespectful cunt. I sound like a bull as streams of hot air come from my nose because I'm breathing so heavily, but my feet stay planted where they are. Hellion steps away from me, looking at my brothers still on the porch when the glint of something streaks through the air.

I hit the deck. "What the fuck?!" I yell, hearing my brothers cuss up a storm behind me. Pushing myself to my feet, I see the smirk on *her* face. My lip curls up in a snarl as I turn and look over my shoulder, eyes narrowing on the shiny object sticking out of the door.

An animalistic roar fills the air, and I whip my head round as Kane yells something incoherent. Hellion has turned feral; her punches are vicious as she attacks the girl. I fold my arms across my chest in anticipation of Hellion finishing this bitch for coming here and doing this. My brows furrow as the fight continues, Ryan meeting Hellion blow for blow.

"What the fuck?" Kane breathes in shock, he comes down to stand at my side as grunts and yells fill the air. The noises catch the attention of the crew as they increase tenfold. They all watch the two women going to town on each other like they can't wait to see the other die.

"Motherhood has made you slow, Reaper," the pink-haired angel of death taunts, then cackles, dancing away from Hellion's blow, her steps are light like she has done this before. "C'mon, I know you can do better than that," she continues to goad her.

"Rip her fucking head off, Hellion," I roar into the air, hoping it's the encouragement she needs to end this shit. The grunts and curses coming from both of them have us all shocked, I don't get it, Hellion's normally ended someone by now.

"C'mon, pretty bird," Kane calls. Liam stands on my other side eagerly watching the shit show in front of us.

"Have you ever seen her take this long to finish someone?" I ask my twin, he trains with her every day, so he is the one who knows her true fighting capabilities better than any of us.

"No, I've never seen her take this long," he says.

I can see the worry shining in his eyes. A roar of pain draws our attention. I stare with my mouth on the floor as Hellion tries her best to get out of the other's hold.

"Tap out," the words are growled as Hellion splutters under her boot. The ferocity on her face even though she's gasping for air has my anxiety spiking. "Tap out, Reaper!"

"Fuck. You," the words come with a savage snarl, she punches Ryan in the kneecap. Her leg gives way instantly and she hits the floor with a thud, and the area is silent as we watch on, waiting to see what happens next.

Manic laughter fills the air as my brothers and I look at one another when another high-pitched manic laugh joins in, making sort of an eerie melody. I watch, stunned, as Hellion pushes herself to her feet, extending a hand out to Ryan on the floor, a huge beaming smile on her face as she looks down at the girl like a long-lost family member. She lifts her to her feet with ease, pulling her into her death grip of a hug as Ryan laughs her head off.

"I've fucking missed you, girl," Hellion says, gripping the pink pixie with a death grip.

"Woah, back the fuck up, Giz!" my twin brother booms, his arms crossing over his chest. Kane mimics his movements, staring down at the newcomer, and all three of us dwarf the two women. But neither of them look bothered by the three pissed-off men glowering at them.

"Plug it, Frosty," Ryan snaps, her eyes narrowing on my brother.

His mouth opens and closes like a fish out of water and I burst out laughing, which is echoed by Ryan, making a shudder pass down my spine. My eyes meet the bluest ones I have ever seen, the feeling intensifying at the contact.

She smirks right back at me as we have some sort of weird showdown, her laughter still echoing through the air. The tinkling sound is cut off when a heartbreaking cry rings out, making my whole body freeze. I shoot off into the house without a backward glance, taking the stairs two at a time and scaring the crap out of the guy who Kane passed my diamond off to. He yelps as I barrel past him to see a head popping over the edge of the cot, and the gut-wrenching sound stops. I scoop her up, bouncing her ever so slightly as she does the biggest yawn ever and snuggles that little bit closer to me. Moments like this make the black tar on my heart crack that little bit more.

"Marcus?" the guard says from the doorway, I turn to face him with a stoic expression. "Boss lady has asked if you can meet them in the kitchen." I make my way out the door and down the corridor with the little bundle of joy in my arms

---

"What're you doing here, Ryan?" Hellion's question stops me in my tracks, I can see around the open doorway but I'm hidden just enough that they can't see me. Rikki is sleeping silently in my arms, as I take a good look at the newcomer for the first time. Fuck me, she's gorgeous, my dick stirs at the thought and I have to stamp out my lust. *Not the time, fuck face, you have your niece in your arms, you knob.*

"I came for a visit, Ri, is that so shocking?" Ryan asks as she grabs a steaming cup off the kitchen island top, bringing it to her lips.

My eyes follow the movement intently, my tongue running across the edge of my lip, wishing I was the rim of the cup.

"Erm, Ri, any reason the pervert is hiding around the wall?" The chuckle that follows has a weird sensation washing over me, but the words hit like a ten-ton truck. I step out of my hiding spot when a squeal splits the air.

"Fucking hell, man, don't wake her up," I snarl at the psycho pink weirdo bouncing across the kitchen to me. She stretches out her arms, a huge smile on her face, and I tuck Rikki in tighter to my chest. "Don't fucking touch her."

The pink pixie cants her head to the side, staring at me, then the bundle in my arms.

"Don't touch her when her Uncle Cheshire has hands on her," Hellion chuckles darkly, while my brothers grumble their agreement. "He's a little protective."

"So␣what're you doing here, pinkie pie?" I ask with a sneer, and Kane glares at me.

I've learned that's his way of telling me not to cause shit while I have a hold of Rikki.

Do I want to know why Ryan's here? Of course I do. So I make my way over and pass Kane his daughter. The lightness I felt with her in my arms instantly disappears and the darkness tugs at the edges of my mind.

"It's not your concern, Cheshire."

2

MARCUS

My mind races with the possibilities of why she would be here, my hands pull at the hair on the top of my head as I pace up and down my room. I had to leave the kitchen because the smug look on the bitch's face had me wanting to rip her head off. She's a danger to us all, I can feel it in my bones. I'm never wrong when I get a feeling like this and no matter how much I do notice her, I have to do the right thing. I need to protect my family.

I have to tell Hellion, she'll believe me. Would she though? From the snippets of conversation I got, they were best friends growing up in boarding school and the pink one took Hellion under her wing. So why would she believe me? They've been friends forever, but then why didn't Hellion call her and ask for help when all the shit went down with Pete? I have to try. I throw the bedroom door open, the wood connecting with the wall with an almighty smack as it ricochets off it.

"Jesus! Fuck?!" one of the grunts shrieks as I step out of my room. "You scared the shit out of me!"

"Where's Hellion?" I snap, not wanting to make idle chit-chat with this dick.

"Office, I think," he stammers, his hand trembling as he points the way to the office like I don't know where the damn thing is. I scoff at his stupidity.

"Fucking idiot," I snarl as I make my way down towards the office. The corridors are quieter than normal and I don't hear my brothers' voices. They're not hard to miss, which tells me if Hellion is in the office, then Kane has Rikki with him and Liam is off doing god knows what. He prefers to spend most of his time at the pit, it's home to him. Plus he won't admit it, but babies freak him out. I remember the first time Hellion passed him his niece so she could do something, I fell off the stool laughing as he held her out at arm's length with terror in his eyes while she cried. In my inner musings, I've worked my way through the house. The office door comes into view and I raise my hand to knock. But my hand freezes mid-air.

"What's the real reason for you coming to visit, Ryan?" Hellion demands, I lean forward slightly, noticing the door is ajar. I quickly have a peak, seeing Hellion sitting behind her desk and Pinkie Pie sitting across from her. I lean back against the wall, stepping sideways as much as I dare so I'm just brushing the edge of the frame.

"I came for a visit, Ri, what's so wrong with that?"

I grind my teeth because I can hear the smirk in her words. The disrespect she has for Hellion annoys the shit out of me, she needs to learn some fucking respect. I have to grip the wall to keep myself from rushing in there and grabbing her by her throat and breaking her fucking neck. Like who the fuck is this bitch?! She comes here like this and…

"Cut the bullshit, Ryan," Hellion snarls, losing her temper. "You and I both know that's a croc, so what the fuck are you doing here?!"

"I stabbed my dad in the eye," the bitch says flippantly.

My mouth drops open at the admission and the room inside goes silent. Hellion being quiet is freaking me out.

"What the fuck do you mean you stabbed your dad in the eye?!" Hellion roars.

I hear the scrape of the office chair flying away from the desk telling me Hellion is on her feet at the admission. "How the fuck are you standing here?"

"Meh," Ryan says.

"Start fucking talking now," Hellion demands. I hear the thwack of what must be her palms on the desk.

"Not a chance when we have someone listening," the other says with a dark chuckle. "My secrets are my own, Reaper, you know that."

My heart stills in my chest as both women go silent, with the corridor being absent of noise it would be possible to hear a pin drop. How the fuck does she know I'm standing here? Nah, man, she has to be bullshitting, she can't know I'm here. I don't do anything other than keep myself firmly pressed against the wall. I look at my feet as the beam of light from the office cuts through the darkness in the corridor, hoping my shadow doesn't show itself to them. Unless she's already seen it.

"Cheshire, get your ass in here!" Hellion demands. I can hear her teeth grinding together, even before I take the step to reveal myself.

"How the fuck did you know I was there?" I question the bitch who just smirks at me.

My lip curls up in a snarl and I glare daggers at her, hoping to see that calm, cool exterior crack but her face is unmoving. My hands are shaking with the overwhelming urge to strangle the bitch, I have to curl my hands into fists

"I can do a lot of things that you couldn't even imagine," she says, her tone thick with sarcasm.

"Watch who you're talking to with that smart mouth of

yours," I demand, losing a semblance of control I'm desperately trying to keep ahold of.

"Or what, Cheshire?" she sneers back, jumping to her feet.

Everything goes black, there's a weird scratching in my head that sounds suspiciously like white noise. I feel my hand has a firm grip on something and a splutter fills my ears as the sounds of the office come back into the forefront of my mind. Then I hear manic laughter as the darkness slowly starts to clear. I see the pink-haired one in my grasp as I squeeze my hand tighter around her throat. Most people have fear clear in their eyes when I lose it like this, but not her. All she does is smirk at me as she pushes forward on my hand.

"Cheshire, let her go!" Hellion screams at me, pulling on my arm. Seeing the smug look on Ryan's face has the darkness within rushing to the surface, begging me to snuff the light out of her.

"She's a danger to us all, Hellion," I snarl, squeezing just a touch harder, hoping to see the fear in her eyes. The look that shines there has the darkness rising even further, it doesn't like to be challenged as much as I do. The snarl that escapes between my lips is more animal than anything.

"Marcus!" I hear my name being called, but I'm too far into the void now. I can feel the tendrils of it tugging me deeper into the blackness. I know from the tone, one of my brothers must have turned up.

"What you going to do, Cheshire?" she sneers at me, and something dances behind her eyes. "C'mon, you know you want to."

She's fucking goading me, has this bitch got a death wish? Would you poke a wild animal when it's backed into a corner? I step closer, lifting her off her feet against the wall, scraping her back against the bricks. I hope it fucking hurts. I stop when the move has brought us to eye level and my lip curls in a snarl as she fucking grins at me.

"Can you do it?" she says. The smile is vicious on her features, and her hand holds onto my wrist as she squeezes it. "Could you snuff me out as easily as blowing out a candle?"

"Don't tempt me," I rumble back. "You may know Hellion but we don't know you, so why the fuck are you here?"

Her lashes flutter against her tanned skin, her eyes dropping our connection. Her breathing becomes heavier as she looks down, minutes feel like they're flying by as I wait to hear her answer because I am not releasing her until I am satisfied that she doesn't pose a threat to me and mine. A sob fills the air, pulling my focus back to her as she lifts her head. Tears pool in the corner of her eyes.

"You're hurting me," she coughs as if her airway is being crushed. "Please stop," she begs again, her face turning ashen and I see sweat begin to bead on her forehead.

Oh fuck! What have I done? I feel the color drain from my face as I stare at her, the pained, terrified look has my stomach rolling. My hand trembles as everything becomes too much.

"I'm sorry," I mutter.

Her head lifts and our eyes connect. The fear that was in her eyes only a second ago has vanished, in its place is pure malice.

I roar as pain spears through my side like an inferno, my hold breaks and she drops to the floor. I stumble back, my hand coming away from my side, red. Blood runs down my fingers as my eyes examine the patch of growing crimson against the white fabric of my t-shirt. My head whips up as I hear a round of oh fucks murmured from everyone in the room. Our eyes connect, and she fucking smirks. She's crouched, a silver blade gleaming against the light, but what draws my attention is the river of crimson running off the tip as I watch my blood drop onto the floor.

My chest rises and falls rapidly as the monster within swarms to the surface, my vision blackens at the edges again. I lunge with a roar and then the room erupts into chaos.

"Liam, grab him!" someone screams, but I don't know who it is, all I can think about is getting my hands on her.

"I'll fucking kill you!" I declare as arms take a firm hold of me, trying to pull me away from her. She doesn't bat an eye at my threat, she stays in the crouch, the blade still on show but the edge of her lip lifts into a nasty grin. "She's going to get us all killed," I bellow to my brothers who now have a hold of me. They both have to adjust their hold to keep pulling me back.

They manage to get me to the door, trying to put as much distance between me and her as they can. She's standing now, and her eyes are dark as she watches me being pulled from the room. Like I'm not the one to be assaulted in my own home.

I grab a hold of the frame, pulling with everything I have to break the hold my brothers have on me and to get my hands on the cunt who is standing at the other side of the room. She hasn't even bothered to put the blade away, my blood still dripping off the end of it. The malice on her face is something the darkness in me doesn't like one fucking bit. She stands tall, smirking at me like I'm some sort of game to her. My brothers heave me out and she disappears from view. I hear the scramble of feet as the other crew members move out of the way.

"Get off me!" I demand, my arms flying as I try and push my brothers' hands off of me. I don't need to be fucking escorted like this.

"Not a fucking chance, brother," Liam snarls as they haul my ass deeper into the house.

"Sit," one of them says before I'm dropped onto a stool, the legs squeaking on the floor as it slides back a little.

"What the fuck was that?" Kane demands as he sits across

from me at the kitchen island. "You know we never willingly hurt a woman?!"

"She dangerous, Kane," I retort. "How can you be so fucking blind to it?"

He studies me like I'm under a fucking microscope. I glare at the pair of them, pissed that they're looking at me like I've lost my mind. It's not often I get a feeling about something but when I do, I am normally right, and my gut is telling me the world we've created is about to go to shit.

"You both know pretty bird wouldn't have anyone here that could harm our way of life," he says as he brushes a hand down his face in exasperation.

"Bu—"

"What the fuck was that?" Hellion demands, striding into the kitchen. She's seething mad, as she glares at me but I don't look at her. My eyes stare firmly on my brothers. I made my point known to her in the office. "Cheshire?"

"Have you put the trash out?" I snipe as I get up and walk to the window, my eyes taking in the area. I hear the bar stools screech against the linoleum and the retreating footsteps of my brothers, leaving me with her.

"She's my friend," she snaps. This is the first time I've ever had Hellion turn her anger on me. Do I regret what I did there? Not a fucking chance.

"A friend? Seriously?!" I scoff. "She's that much of a good friend to you that you never mentioned her once, and then this so-called friend just turns up!" I bellow, spinning to face her. "Don't you understand how I find that weird?"

"No!" she fires back, her eyes narrowed on me as she folds her arms across her chest. "I always told her, no matter when or where, I would be there if she needed me."

"Ask yourself why is she here, Hellion?" I say, mimicking her stance, folding my arms across my chest and leaning against the kitchen side. "She stabbed her fucking dad in the eye, then shows up like she's on some fancy vacation or some shit. But she stabbed her father!"

"Look!" she snaps. "I know everything about her. I know she came here because I told her I would be there for her, no matter what." She blows out a harsh breath, I can see the anger contained within her from her red face. "I get what she did, but trust me when I say the shit I went through looks like a fairy tale compared to the things she's had to endure."

I open my mouth to retort and she puts a hand up, effectively cutting me off.

"Her story is her own to tell, but she is my friend and I am here for her," her voice softens just a touch. "All I'm asking of you is to trust me."

"I do trust you, it's her I don't," I say, relaxing a little. I may have my brothers, but Hellion is my family too. "Because you asked, I won't throw her ass out just yet. Make no mistake though, Hellion. If shit hits the fan, she's out of here faster than you could ever imagine."

"Thank you," she says as she steps up to me. She wraps her hands around me, pulling me into a hug. "I have to go and do some errands, could you please try not to kill my friend?"

"I'm not making that promise," I say with an evil smirk.

3

RYAN

Fuck my life, I shouldn't have come here. I didn't realize Ri had managed to get a hold of her life. She's happy and I know the shit show that's about to come is going to upset her status quo. I can't do that to her. Plus, the one who gripped hold of me sees more than a stranger should.

My fingers brush against my neck, tracing where his fingers dug into my throat like I can still feel his fingers against me. I can't help myself. I've never wanted to push someone as much as I do him, the demons in the depths of his soul are easily seen. Even the darkness within me stood up and paid attention. I've never met anyone who could share the same darkness as me. I thought I was the only one, a product of my environment. It makes me wonder what sort of life he has had, as well as the others. Do they truly know the depths of what Reika has been through?

I never thought Ri would ever be a mother, she always seemed too hard to be able to take care of something so fragile. But seeing the way she is with her daughter, and how damn cute the little girl is, even my cold heart melted a touch.

They're going to come for me, I know it. There is no way

my father or his generals will let me get away with what I did. But even being the killer that I am, I have my limits so when he ordered me to kidnap the child of a politician, I refused. He thought getting more than thirty people to beat me and starve me in the holding cell would make me change my mind. Ha, he learned the hard way.

They say blood is thicker than water, but I say your family is who you choose and I see Ri as a part of my family.

The decision is made, and I grab my backpack. Glad I didn't unpack anything from the meager belongings I had a chance to grab. I check the huge clip of cash is still where I put it, I wouldn't want to have to hunt down whichever idiot from the crew decided to steal it.

I stick my head out of the door, looking both ways down the corridor before I slip out and move to the front door. I can hear her and the one she calls Cheshire talking as I slip past the kitchen, making sure the front door closes softly behind me.

Am I sneaking out? Kinda, I'm not good at goodbyes and I'm not sure if I will see her again.

4

MARCUS

The reflection staring back at me in the mirror is something I didn't think I would see so soon. The darkness shines in my eyes as I roll the cuffs of my black shirt over my elbows, making sure they're both the same size. Brushing my hands down the front of the shirt, I try and push some small creases out. I left the conversation with Hellion still as annoyed as I was to begin with, and my mood soured more having to have doc stitch me back up. He was shocked to find out the pink pixie managed to stab me.

I know she's somewhere in the house, Hellion went looking for her so after I got stitched up, I came up here to get ready to head to the Den. After my diamond was born, I thought Hellion would want control of all her assets back, we all did. But no, she said she's happy to oversee everything and stay with Rikki.

My black jeans and sneakers match my shirt. Kane asked me when I first came down in this one day why I wasn't wearing slacks, but I shut that shit straight down. He may like to stroll around in a suit and do the whole power play thing but me, I think this because it doesn't show blood as easily and they're easily replaced if I need to burn them.

Grabbing my keys from the side of my bed, I head out of my room, making sure the door is locked before I walk down the stairs and head out. I can hear a commotion and Hellion barking orders. I shrug as I grab the door handle on the front door and it swings open. A grunt stands there with fear etched on his face as I growl at him.

"Cheshire?" Hellion says from behind me, and I look over my shoulder. "Have you seen Ryan?" she asks. I shake my head but don't move at the look on her face. "She gone."

"Good," I say and push past the grunt, my car firmly in my sights.

I climb into the car and she stands there watching me as I turn the engine on and pull out. The worry etched on her face gets smaller as she becomes but a blip in the distance.

Carnal Desires is in full swing as I walk to the front doors. The security guards nod at me and I hear a few of the customers lined up booing at me. I turn and look at a guy whose face pales instantly as I stare him down. A smirk twitches the corner of my mouth as he rushes through an apology and tries to drag his party away with him.

"How are we doing in there?" I ask as I follow the line of people waiting to get in, my eyes widening as I see the line goes all the way to the end of the block before it disappears around the corner.

"Full house, Boss," my head of security says. "It's been quiet on the brawling front too."

This is a surprise, most people here get into something within an hour of the place opening and I'm nearly two hours late this evening. But that's not a problem, every member of staff knows if I'm not here, they have to act like I am.

Hopefully, we can have a drama-free night and another girl won't quit on me.

I head in through the black doors and I'm swallowed by the dark corridor that's illuminated with a pulsing red light. Catcalls and wolf whistles come from inside as I push through the thick black curtain.

London twists and turns around the pole on the main stage. All the people sitting at the tables in the circle surrounding it are glued to the sensual experience going on. I head over to the bar, nodding my head in approval as the bartender slides my drink of choice down to me. A customer growls something about favoritism and I give him a friendly smile and head to the door that says employees on it.

The dancers are laughing and joking with one another as I pass the dressing room and stick my head in. Just so they know I'm here now as I know most of them prefer to come and talk to me than the manager Caleb, who is one of the crew members. But it's been pretty obvious since day one of him being here the girls don't like him. I only keep him around because his ideas bring a shit load of traffic to the club.

"Hey, Marcus," Raven says with a sultry tone, her eyes raking up and down the length of my body. I smirk at the lust shining in her eyes. "Looking good, Boss."

"Fucking hell, Raven, put the pheromone levels down a notch. Your desperate is showing," Candice smirks.

"Fuck you, bitch!" Raven screeches, rushing towards the other girl. I move quickly, blocking her off from the other stripper, and her eyes lift to mine.

"I do not condone fighting between my girls, if you want to brawl, take it to the pit!" I snap, my head taking in all the girls' eyes widening and they shake their heads.

I turn my attention back to Raven. Her face is so tense it looks like she has a lemon in her mouth. My eyes narrow on her until I see her anger start to slip away. I lift my hand, brushing my thumb across her cheek and she melts into the touch, her eyes becoming glassy. "I have told you this already, I like the enthusiasm but I don't screw my girls."

"Sorry," she mumbles, her eyes on the floor. I have to glare at a couple of the girls who snigger under their breath. Raven isn't liked much by the other girls, and I think that boils down to the fact she won't accept the fact I won't fuck her. The only reason I keep her here is because she is one of the best dancers and the influx of customers when she is on stage makes the dollar signs flash in my head.

"You all good for the rest of the night?" I ask, stepping back to the door.

"Yep," echoes as the girls answer in unison.

They all smile at me as I nod. Spinning on my heels I head out of the dressing room and down the corridor toward the office. The door flies open as I push it, and a screech fills the air so high-pitched I wince. A blonde woman stumbles around on the highest heels I've ever seen as she scrambles to collect her clothing.

"Marcus!" The words are higher than they should be coming from any man. I fold my arms across my chest, glaring at the guy who is frantically trying to do up his fly. "Sorry, man."

"Fucking sorry?" I snarl as my eyes take in the strewn paperwork and laptop that are haphazardly laid around on the floor. "You use my fucking office as a fuck pad? Are you for real, Caleb?"

"I…" His words break off and I see the sweat start to gather on his brow.

"Get out of here now!" I snarl at the woman who doesn't think twice, she rushes out the door without bothering to put her clothes back on. "My fucking office."

"Marcu—"

"Shut the fuck up!" His mouth slams shut. "I offered you this job because you proved yourself in the crew the night we got Hellion back, but this much disrespect? If any of my shit is damaged, I will fuck you up."

"Bu—"

"Get the fuck out!"

Caleb rushes out the door while fastening the buttons and shit on his shirt. I glare as I take in the room. They must have been so desperate to fuck that they cleared off the entire contents of my desk in one swipe of an arm. I swear to god, is it something in the water or something, because all the single crew members have been wanting to fuck like rabbits for the last few days.

"*Maybe you should try to get laid too!*" my inner voice snarks, my spine snapping straight as I hear the voice laughing in my head. I rush to the adjoining bathroom and practically rip the damn medicine cabinet off the wall in my haste to get the door open.

The medicine bottles fall out into the sink, I grab them, desperately trying to find the one I need. I fucking knew I had forgotten something this morning with the pink pixie turning up! I spot the bottle I want and grab hold of it, twisting the cap off and tip my dose onto the palm of my hand.

"*We're not that bad! Why do you want to get rid of us so much?!*" the voice croons as I stare at my reflection.

"Shut up!" I snarl at the mirror. "Shut the fuck up. You're the reason I do the shit I do!"

"*But am I though, or am I showing you what you're truly capable of being?*" it cackles. I throw the tablet into my mouth and swallow it, my chest rising and falling rapidly. I grab the edge of the sink, my grip so tight I'm shocked the porcelain isn't cracking.

Why have they decided to show up now? I don't need to be having anther fucking episode with everything going on. Fuck! If Hellion finds out that I'm hearing them again, she's going to be heartbroken. I only went to the doctor to get some help because of her and Diamond, I want to be the best uncle I can be to that little girl.

I do the breathing exercises Hellion taught me as I lean on the sink. Waiting, I can hear the voices becoming quieter in my head as they ease off. I'm able to stand up straight and see myself now; the dark circles under my eyes, the sweat on my forehead from the panic I felt hearing it for the first time in a few weeks.

My breathing is a little easier and I release the death grip I have on the sink. Brushing my hand down my face, I don't bother picking the other bottles up. I head back into the office and start clearing up.

5

MARCUS

My fingers fly over the keys as I work through all the business admin I've been left to do. I'm seriously going to have to rethink Caleb's employment status here after seeing the shit show of everything he's left in his wake. The office is pure chaos, papers are piled high and the figures on the accounts look like a child's done them. Honestly, if I notice any money missing from any transactions, my mental state is that temperamental right now I would more than likely rip his head off and not think twice about it.

The numbers on the screen begin to swirl together as my eyes dance between the laptop and the iPad laid on my desk, making sure all the numbers match up. I'm impressed with how much the business has grown since I took over, and I know the others appreciate it. Hellion didn't think twice when she put each of us in charge of one of the businesses she *acquired* should we say. I was happy as a pig in shit with getting this place though. Don't get me wrong, I would have been happy with any of them but…

My excitement may have something to do with the number of drunken nights I've spent here when the shit in my head became too much. My eyes keep jumping to the huge TV screens lining the walls that give me free access to see all the comings and goings in the building. A shadow catches my eye, and I zone in on the screen which shows the corner of the club, closest to the women's toilets. The person turns and my heart drops into my stomach.

"No fucking way?!"

I jump to my feet, abandoning everything. My mind is playing the image over and over in my head as I stride out of the office. Disbelief mixes with rage as the eyes that have been haunting me glow in my mind's eye. No! It can't be, my mind must be playing tricks on me again. I fucking hope it is, because I don't want to think about what's going to happen if it's not.

The door flies open, making a couple of guys standing to the side shriek. I burst out, my eyes scanning the area looking for her I'm a man on a mission, there is no way she's getting out of here; I can't believe she would be that fucking stupid to come back. I push through groups of people; I get to the area where I saw her on the camera but it's empty. My circle is small as I turn around to see if I can find her in the mass of people.

"Everything okay, Boss?" Caleb's nasally tone asks from my side.

"I'm looking for someone I saw on the camera," I say, standing on the booth seat to give myself the high advantage. I'm tall but the crowd in here now is fucking huge. I shouldn't be looking like this, standing here looking over the crowd, but even though I'm tall I can't see over the full length of the room with this many people. I'm praying the little bitch doesn't see me.

"Who?" he asks, turning towards me. I can see the curiosity in his eyes. I glare at him, my lip curling up into a snarl. He throws his hands up and gulps as I step down, still towering over him. "It's all good, man, I'm curious, that's all."

My eyes are scanning the crowd, the neon lights causing havoc with my vision. But I push through, that's when I spot her. I rush through the crowd towards the bar, shoving people out of my way. I get to where she was standing, but the spot is empty. A drink is on the bar, but the owner is no longer here. My head whips around, maybe she went outside? I head out, trying to see if she's hiding in the alcoves of the dark entrance hallway.

She would do that, just to fucking toy with me. That's the only explanation I have as to why she would come back. She wants to fuck with my head! That must be it, the bouncer nods as I step out of the door. My head whips left and right as I look up and down the street but there is no sign of her. The wind has picked up a chill now, and I scoff because, just like that, she is gone. Again!

The rage spills over, and I spin. My fist connects with the wall at the side of the door. A few people from the line shriek as some of the brick crumbles loose. A throbbing builds in my knuckles, but I use the sensation to ground me here and now, in this moment. What the fuck is she playing at? Why the fuck would she come here? I rub my head as the images play over in my mind, I went to the bar where I saw her but it was empty. A lone drink that could have been left by anybody was all that remained; did I see her or is my mind some sort of twisted game with me once again?

"You okay, Boss?" I turn to the voice, his eyes widening as his eyes drop to my knuckles.

I can feel the blood running down my fingers, everything narrows on the blood, but I don't give a shit. The throbbing has intensified to a stabbing pain, I'm pretty sure I broke something. It's hard to explain, I can feel it but it's like it's muted as everything runs through my mind. I really need to try and clean myself up though because Hellion is going to lose it when she sees me, and so is Doc come to think of it. He was chastising me like a father would a child earlier, saying I'm the only crew member he has stitched up so many times he's surprised I'm not made up of scar tissue. I pull my phone out and swipe until I find the picture.

"If this bitch comes near here again, radio for me straight away and don't let her in," I snarl, my anger is hellish as the thought crosses my mind on how many more times is she going to show her face before disappearing into the dark.

"Got it, but she hasn't been here tonight," he says with a frown.

"What?" My brows hit my hairline. "I've just seen her on the cameras inside."

"Could it have been someone who looks like her?" he asks.

"No, it was her!"

My mind's racing, could it have been someone that looks like her? No, I know what I saw. His eyes are glued to me as he waits for me to say something, his eyes suspicious like I'm losing my fucking mind. Fuck this. If he doesn't want to believe me, I'm not bothering to try and convince him.

With a growl of frustration, I turn on my heels and practically rip the door open before striding down the hallway. My already shitty mood drops to dangerous levels. The beat of the music makes the floor pulse under my feet, and I know Raven has taken the stage. The customers lose it as I walk through the door into the main floor. My eyes on the bar, I walk over and take in all the liquor on the top shelf.

"What you after, Boss?" My vision is swimming, I can't make anything out as the lights and my mood have multi-colored dots bouncing in front of my eyes like there's a party in my head.

"Whiskey," I say as he nods and grabs a glass. "No, I want the fucking bottle."

He cringes but gives me the bottle without protest, I grab it by the neck and skulk my way to a darkened corner with an available table. I drop into my seat, bringing the bottle to my lips. My hand wraps around the neck of the bottle in a death. Am I wishing it was someone's neck? Totally, but I'll have to wait for her to show her face again, when she does, I will be ready. My phone vibrates in my pocket and I lean forward, pulling it out. I chuckle when I see Hellion pop up on the screen with an incoming message.

HELLION

Any particular reason why you punched a wall? x

ME

Nope, who snitched? x

HELLION

Does it matter? What did the wall do so wrong to you, Cheshire? x

ME

I'm all good, Hellion! You don't need to worry about me, okay? Trust me, I'm fine, have you found your friend yet? x

HELLION

Nope, she's dropped off the face of the earth again. She'll be back x

ME

What makes you so sure of that? x

My curiosity is peaked, I can tell by the way the message is written that she is deadly sure about her pink-haired pixie coming back. Personally, good fucking riddance, my gut is still churning with the impending doom it was feeling.

HELLION
She's found a new toy to play with lol ;) x

An influx of bodies catches my peripheral, I lift my head. My eyes narrow on the mass of people crowded around the center stage as a sensual beat plays and all the guys whoop and catcall. Hmm, I wonder who's on stage? Raven can't be back out already? Shit, have I been sitting here that long? Pushing to my feet, I grab the now half-empty bottle of whiskey. I rub my hand down my face, and suddenly, for some reason, I feel tired. But needs must so I should get my ass back to work, no point stressing over whether I actually saw her or not.

In the first step I take, I sway precariously as the whole room spins like I'm on a fairground ride, and I snort a laugh. Oh fuck! This shit is strong. I look at the bottle and my vision swims again. I chuckle as I pour some more of it down my neck, stumbling out from behind the table. Shit! Alcohol never bothers me like this, what the fuck?! It takes all my concentration to be able to put one foot in front of the other without falling face-first. I make it to the bar when a flash of color catches my eye. I whip around so fucking fast my eyes feel like they're rolling in my head.

"The fuck?!" I dig the heel of my palms into my eye sockets, trying to clear this damn fog and to be certain my eyes aren't playing tricks on me again. My vision clears and the picture is still happening in front of me.

The noise of the crowd is getting louder, my eyes catch on the dancers standing off to the side, all their arms are folded as they glare at the unwelcome body on the stage. The crowd is going wild. I stride forward; I can see Caleb trying to catch someone's attention.

"Get down off my fucking stage now!" My voice booms and the DJ instantly cuts the music.

"No."

My teeth grind together at the defiance slung my way. I jump up onto the stage, stopping the spin on the pole as I grab hold of her by her waist and haul her ass over my shoulder.

The crowd boo me as I jump down off the stage, impressed with how I managed to land on my feet in this drunken state. I stride past the end of the bar, grab the half-empty bottle, and bring it with me as I push through the office door. It slams shut behind us, and I can still hear the complaints of the customers. But it doesn't take long for the music to start again and the boos turn to cheers. I throw her ass down in the seat in front of my desk.

"What the fuck are you doing in my club?" I demand, folding my arms across my chest as I glare at the bitch I was hoping to never see again.

"Aww, what's the matter? Didn't you like the show?" Her words are slurred as she slumps in her chair, her body so low it's on her tailbone.

"Cut the shit, Pinkie Pie!" I bellow, grabbing the bottle and guzzling the contents in one breath. My head swims as I sway from side to side. "Hellion has been looking for you, she thought you left but you end up here?"

"I did, but then I got really thirsty, so I decided to go for a drink," she says flippantly. "The rest… well you saw how that went."

"Stripping, in my club of all fucking places," I fire back. "Will you put your fucking clothes back on?" I snarl as I drop into my office chair.

I open the drawer on the right of me and pull out a shitty cheap bottle of liquor that Caleb thinks I didn't know was hidden there. The seal breaks with a sweet crunch as I twist off the cap and drink straight from the bottle.

"Don't let the door hit you on the ass on the way out," I say as I wipe my hand across my mouth.

"Who were you looking for earlier?" she asks out of the blue.

The blood in my veins freezes instantly as she leans forward, she's still half naked, only in her underwear. She cocks her head to the side, a weird look on her face like she's studying a bit of bacteria in a microscope. The voices start a chant instantly. I cover my ears to try and block them out as I feel the darkness twisting at my insides, desperate to claw its way to the surface.

"Wow, whoever it is must really get under your skin," she chuckles.

"Get out," I snarl, my hands are still over my ears as I try and take slow breaths in hopes it passes. "Get out, now!" I bellow, but I don't hear or feel any movement of her leaving.

"Why?" My head whips up at her voice, my eyes widening when I find her sitting on the desk in front of me. Her gaze is curious as she looks me over. "Why do you hide it?"

"What?" I snarl through my panting.

The darkness is fighting with everything it has and, in my drunken state, it's winning. I close my eyes trying to ground myself, conjuring up the images of everything I hold dear. The memories of my family as we laugh and joke in the kitchen, how happy we finally are, and Hellion and Diamond are safe.

"Why do you fight it so hard?" she asks, leaning closer our noses are almost touching.

"You should leave now before I hurt you!" I snarl.

She throws her head back and laughs her ass off. That fuels the darkness within, it rushes to the surface like an inferno I'm not able to hold back.

A soft touch on my hand has me pulling away, she's standing in between my legs looking down at me as she moves my hands away from my ears. Her smile is different from the feral looks I've seen on her face. She pushes forward and I freeze as she climbs onto my lap, straddling me.

"Why do you hide it?" she asks again. She's so close I can feel her hot breath on my cheek like a soft caress. "Hiding only makes it worse."

My head tilts back, craning as far away from her as I can. My eyes narrow as I get a closer look at her eyes, my mouth dropping open in surprise as I see the darkness swirling in her eyes. They're the same as mine every time I look in the mirror.

"Get off me, Ryan," I snarl, pushing her backward. Her grip tightens on the top of the chair keeping her in place. "I'm not the sort of person you want to be toying with."

"I can handle it," she whispers against my ear, her scent wrapping around my other senses. The darkness is clawing at me more perversely, waiting to rise to the challenge. "I think you know I can."

The defiance and darkness shining in her eyes calls to my own, and my hand wraps around her throat, pulling her close. Our breaths mingle together, and lust flashes in her eyes at the sound building in the back of my throat. I open my mouth, words on the tip of my tongue. But I stop myself, the feel of her soft, plump lips tenderly brushing against mine.

"I'm not doing this shit again," I snarl, shoving her hard again. She yelps as she slides off my legs and ends up in a heap on the floor.

"What the fuck?!" she booms, jumping to her feet.

"Get the fuck out!" I snarl, turning the chair so the back of it is facing her.

Carnal Desires is consumed by darkness as the lights go out. The customers slowly dwindled into the night and, honestly, I'm in such a bad mood I told the girls they could go home earlier. The staff helped me clean up and then they left, meaning I'm the last one in the building, but that doesn't bother me. I need to take some time to myself and get my head clear.

I don't know how or why but, for some reason, the pink pixie gets under my fucking skin, I've never wanted to choke someone out and fuck them at the same time so much.

The street is silent at this time of night, I have to smile seeing the breeze take the litter and swirl it around. Everyone is normally repulsed by how much this side of the city is in disrepair, but I really don't give a shit. It's home, we do our best for the people, Hellion is heading up a couple of outreach programs for kiddies and pushing as much cash into businesses and anything else she can to help.

I climb into my car, my hands running across the leather of the wheel as I take a deep breath.

What the hell is with me and all the nostalgia tonight? I haven't got a clue; I think her question is really getting to me because that's the first time anyone has ever asked me that. Why do I hide it? I do it because of Diamond, Hellion, and my brothers. I don't want them to see how far the darkness truly goes. My Diamond is the only thing that keeps me afloat, seeing her little face, the innocence. Nothing and no one will ever put that in jeopardy.

6

RYAN

The replay in my mind's eye of him shoving me off his legs has me cackling to myself as I sit beside the window in my room in the crew house, staring out into the darkness beyond. I've never been much of a sleeper, but the older I get the worse it gets. So, I think, by this point, I'm more of an insomniac if I'm being honest. I don't even feel tired like I normally would after being up for nearly seventy-two hours. That's how long it's taken for me to get here and avoid the fuckers I know are chasing me down.

Shit! I bet they tried to be hot on my heels as soon as I got out of my garage, I stopped at random places before doubling back and coming here.

Demon was right when he told her I would bring hell here, I told Ri everything after I got back from the strip club. I apologized for possibly bringing a shit show to her door, but I haven't been in contact with her enough for my father to notice so I'm hoping he doesn't think to come here. Although, with that fucker, I never know. I was surprised when Ri told me we would deal with it if the time came.

Then we sat for the first time ever and I filled her in on all the details she doesn't know since we left boarding school. I also apologized for not staying in contact as much, and the best thing about her is that she understood.

Her father was a fucker, just like my own. Well, I always thought he was until she told me everything, I missed with her. Which pissed me off considering, if she had reached out, I would have come to help without a thought. We got so lost in the conversation, before we both knew it dawn had come around.

I'm glad we did it though, it was nice to have someone who understands having a twisted sociopath for a parent.

After our little heart to heart, she told me to stay. I can breathe a little easier knowing she understands why I did what I did. I rest my head against the window, and the coolness of the glass has my mind wandering.

"Your father wants to see you now, Harbinger." My head turns to look at the asshole my father calls his second, I glare at him as he stands there all high and mighty in his slick, tailored suit, glaring at me like I'm a disobedient child. "Move it! He has a job for you."

The growl in his tone has me jumping to my feet and I smile slightly as he steps back, making sure to keep as much distance between us as he can.

"Lead the way," I snark with a flamboyant wave of my hand.

He shakes his head at me but never turns his back, which has the smile widening on my face. What a clever little maggot, I cock my head and run my eyes up and down his body, taking him in—purely just to piss him off a little bit more. I've been cooped up in here now for nearly three months and I'm going out of my damn mind.

"Are you going to behave yourself?" he asks, his eyes as sharp as knife points as he watches me.

"Of course!" I drawl. "When am I anything less than perfectly behaved?"

"I'm not playing these games, Ryan. Your father wants to see you. Now!" he snaps. I smirk as he turns his back on me, his strides are long and powerful as he covers the ground quickly.

My laughter fills the air as I skip after him, a beaming smile on my face, when someone I don't recognize steps out of an adjoining corridor. He slams to a stop, his eyes widening as I pause in front of him, my head cocking to the side. I hear. "Oh fuck," muttered behind him, and I lean slightly to the left to see around his body, cackling as I see one of the newer soldiers looking like he's about to haul ass out of here.

"Dude, don't move," he says, my attention gets drawn back to the newest one who just spoke. I see the slight jarring movement of his foot and my eyes zero in on it.

"Don't fucking move," the other says.

"I'd do as he says," I purr, stepping up to the new guy so we are chest to chest. I'm smaller than everyone here but that doesn't pose a problem for me. "What's ya name?" I ask, running the edge of my nail across his jawline, it snags every now and then on his stubble.

"Ryan!" my father's voice booms through the corridor. I turn just enough to keep the newbie in front of me, but my attention is firmly on my father, who has now emptied the entire corridor. "Get your ass here, now."

"I want to play with him." I pout, looking back at the new guy. "He's pretty." I can see the tremble of his body.

"I…" His words break off; I smile at him because even the small word tells me he has a deep tone to his voice, and I like that a lot.

"Ryan?!"

"Fucking hell, I'm coming, keep your damn hair on!" I snarl, my eyes narrowed on my father's at the far end of the corridor. His arms are folded across his chest as he glares at me. "Come find me later if you want to play?" I say to the newbie, before turning my attention away from him reluctantly and striding down the corridor. I'm not in the mood to skip anymore, fucking asshole always ruins my fun.

He takes off in front of me, his strides strong and sure as we get to the end of the corridor. He steps into the meeting room, which is filled with his general and the lieutenants, they all turn and nod their heads to my father as he takes his place at the head of the table.

Malik sits on his side, with the arrogant air wafting everywhere from him. God, I hate that asshole. He looks over at me, the disgust clear in his eyes. I flip him off and make my way to the chair that has been set up for me behind my father. The lieutenants look me over as I drop into the seat, making me chuckle darkly. They're all blind to the fact that they have put me here for their safety, not my own.

"Why is my daughter seated behind me?" my father's gruff tone cuts through the room, commanding all eyes to turn in his direction. Malik shuffles at his side as I smirk, waiting eagerly for someone to answer.

"Well, Boss, we're here to discuss all matters," Malik says, while playing with the perfectly laid tie around his neck.

"I sent your brother to get her as this meeting involves her, and you stick her there?" he growls out of the corner of his mouth. I burst out laughing as one of the lieutenants jumps to his feet and grabs another chair.

He carries it the length of the table and puts it three seats away from my father, the others all shuffle down the line to make space for me. I push to my feet, my eyes connecting with each person in the room, and I spot Malik glaring at me as I take my seat. The guy next to me shuffles further down and I laugh.

"You all know we've constantly had a problem with people paying the money that is owed to me, and we've had to show force on more than one occasion." My father's voice is firm as he fills in the others on the issues. I tuned everything out, examining my fingernails out of boredom as nothing piques my interest.

"Harbinger?" My head lifts to meet my father's eyes, I raise a brow at the god-awful nickname he gave me when I was younger. Does it hold power in this world? Yes. Do I hate it with a fucking passion? Hell yes. I hate that they all see me as his weapon, not his daughter. "Politician Adams is being rather reluctant to the deal we made, so I need you to send him a reminder."

"Okay," I say, sitting up a little straighter. "Who do you want me to hurt? His brother?"

"I want you to kidnap his son," he says, his gaze firm.

My heart practically stops in my chest as I'm rendered speechless for the first time ever. His cold, calculating eyes never leave mine as I stare at him, my mind trying to work out what the hell is going on.

"He's had plenty of time to remedy this situation, but now he is doing this deliberately. So you will kidnap his son and if he doesn't cooperate, I want you to ki—"

"You want me to murder a child?!" My anger fills the room as I jump to my feet. "A fucking child!"

My breathing is erratic and I stare at the only family I have left; he can't be serious. I know he's twisted in the head but even *he* wouldn't go so far with it, would he? I wait, hoping and praying that he tells me this is some sort of twisted joke.

"Have you finished?" he asks with a sneer. "You have your orders."

"Tell me you're joking?!" I demand, pushing away from the table, my head whipping around to the other men in the room. All of them look unfazed by what my father is asking me to do. "You can't be fucking serious?"

My eyes are wide as I take him in, my eyes drilled in on any slight little movement he makes, I'm looking for any tell that he is lying because what sort of person no matter who you are could condone hurting a child? He doesn't bat an eye at my outburst, I knew he was a bad person. Hell, I've always known and I followed closely in his footsteps, but this? I can see the monster he truly is, no matter the amount of blood that stains my hands.

"I won't do it!" I declare, my tone thick with determination. "This isn't right."

"You're my daughter," he sneers, the look of disgust on his face as my anger rises. "You have been trained to follow my every command, you took an oath, Harbinger."

"I remember it well, but I never signed up for this," I throw back, my voice louder than his. "You are so desperate to bring everyone under your iron grip that you would do the unimaginable?!"

"Collateral damage." My mouth hits the floor as he shrugs it off like it's just a normal thing for him. I can see by the set of his jaw that he won't change his mind but now this has given me more questions. How many kids have been hurt in his quest for power and wealth? "If you don't follow your order, you will suffer the consequences."

I cock my head to the side, taking everything in. The

lieutenants have moved away from the table, the door tried to open silently but I caught it as a handful of soldiers stepped into the room.

"So what're you planning on doing then?" he asks, his tone void of emotion.

I know anyone seeing this shit going down would be asking if he would really hurt his only child. Unfortunately, the answer is yes.

I am a product of my environment. The training and stuff that would give people nightmares I've had to endure at the hands of him and his men. Well, it shapes a person. I stand tall, taking in every factor in the room, my eyes bouncing from all the Lieutenants to the soldiers that are trying to keep themselves in the shadows. Blowing out a harsh sigh, I see the edge of my father's lips twitch.

My knees bend, and his face splits into a triumphant grin. I launch myself up, my feet hitting the table as I dash across it. I roar in anger as I launch off the edge, the switchblade firmly in my grasp. His brows raise in fear and I drive it home into his right eye socket. He hits the floor and I don't think as the room erupts into chaos. The sound of guns being fired has me covering my head, things smashing all around me as I charge to the window. I jump, tightening the hold on my head as the window smashes from the force of my body.

"Ryan?"

My eyes flutter as the memory disappears and I'm pulled back into the present. I look over my shoulder to the door, my brows scrunching together in a frown when I see Ri's other half standing there like a mountain. The dark look in his eyes tells me he would rather be anywhere else than standing at the threshold of my room. "Reika needs your help with something."

I nod, climbing off the window seat and shove my feet into my boots. Grabbing the hoodie as I pass the bed, I tug it over my head and step out into the hallway. Kane's waiting at the top of the stairs, and he turns to walk down them as I approach. I follow him towards the office—I know it's the office because it's the only place I know how to get to in here.

Kane opens the door for me and then steps aside so I can go in first. There are people everywhere, but the three that stand out are Ri as she stands behind the desk, the other twin leaning against the wall to my right, and one of the seats in front of the desk is occupied—and I know who it is without having to see him.

"Thanks for coming, Ryan," Ri says with a smile.

"What's she doing here?" Demon growls, looking over his shoulder, his lip curling up. Then he turns his attention back onto Ri. "This is Crew business."

"Put a cork in it, will you?" I snap at him. I walk over to the empty chair and drop down, smirking as he shuffles his seat further away from me. Did I sit here to piss him off? Hell yeah.

"For fuck sake!" she booms, her hands hitting the desk. Her eyes narrow on me before jumping to him, then back to me… "Will you both put a sock in it? Fuck my life," she says, shaking her head. "You do know, you two only hate each other so much because you're exactly the same."

"I'm fuck all like her," Demon snarls to my right, the disdain dripping from every word.

"I'm better looking," I say with a chuckle, and I hear someone bark out a laugh, trying to cover it up with a cough.

"Fuck you!" he bellows, jumping to his feet.

"Your room or mine?" I retort, chuckling as his eyes widen

just a touch. Then, the oh-so-scary mean man face slips over his features.

"I've got a job I need doing," Ri says before he can say anything else. This piques my interest, I ignore his bitching as I turn all my attention on her. Ri glares at him for another couple of minutes until his muttering stops. I can feel eyes on the side of my head but I pay him no mind. "Cheshire, I need you to do what you do best."

"Who?" he asks eagerly, leaning forward in his seat.

"Jamieson Ashton, he's been causing a lot of issues for us recently. He's also trying to gain a foothold in the town by creating his own crew," she says with a growl. Even I lean closer at this tid-bit of information. Why would someone want to try anything here? Ri's reputation is legendary and, I have to admit, even the guys have one too.

"How far you want me to go, Hellion?" he asks, his tone filled with excitement. I turn to look at him and I can see the pure joy and darkness in his eyes. Damn, maybe we are more similar than we thought.

"Drag it out, then do what you do best, Cheshire." The stoic look on her face is kind of terrifying, well, for your everyday Joe, but I know her and I know there is more going on than she's letting on. "Also me and Kane are going away tonight with Rikki for a few weeks."

"No, you're not taking Diamond," Demon shouts from my side, jumping to his feet in an outburst. I find my gaze is drawn to him more and I see fear flash in his eyes.

"Really, Bro?" Kane growls from behind her. "Of course we are taking our daughter!" He folds his massive arms across his chest as he glares at his brother. My head bounces between the pair of them before I catch the sad look in Ri's eyes. They don't know her like I do, and I can tell she's feeling guilty for some reason.

"Cheshire?" she says calmly, rounding the desk and standing in front of him. I hold back the giggle at them, because damn, it's a funny picture. He towers over her, she has to crane her neck back to look at him. "Reed's called in a favor so I have to go and help him out. You will be fine here."

"You know that's not true," he whispers, his voice so low I think I'm the only other person who heard his words. The sadness and fear there tug at my little black heart. Why's he so worried that they're leaving?

"I know you can do this," she says, pulling him into a hug, "If it gets too bad, you need to ask Ryan for help."

He pulls back, his eyes wide as he stares at her in disbelief. His blue irises meet mine and I can see the shimmer of something flitting across his gaze. His face is deathly pale, and I notice the tremble in his hands as he grips onto the back of her t-shirt.

"No!" he says, the sound like a child on the verge of throwing a tantrum. "I'm not asking anyone for help, especially not her."

He storms out of the room, everyone staring after him. Someone yelps and then I hear his feet hitting the stairs. His door slams... then there is silence. All I see is sadness when I look at my friend, Ri. She turns to address Kane.

"I'm not so sure this is a good idea," she says, stepping into his outstretched arms, and he pulls her into his chest, hugging her. "He's unstable, big man, and I don't want to think about what could go wrong."

"I'll keep an eye on him," I offer, both their eyes widen as they stare at me in disbelief. Yeah, that just surprised me too, but I can see the fear she has and if I can do something to help her, I will. "I promise he'll be fine."

"We really appreciate the offer, Ryan, but my brother is..."

His words break off like he's trying to find the right way to say it.

"Consumed with darkness?" I ask, my arms folded. "He has demons that make him react violently when they start tormenting him? He doesn't sleep, becomes highly volatile, and the doctors have prescribed him all sorts of medication to keep them at bay?"

Both of them stare at me, their jaws on the floor as I watch them. This would be comical normally, but I can see how worried they are.

"He struggles with the urges when they start, which makes him terrifying to people, but when he has a hold of Rikki or he knows she's close it helps him keep his cool?"

"How did you know?" Kane breathes in surprise. "Nobody knows."

"Ri knows my secrets are my own. But when she said to him we are one and the same, she wasn't lying," I say with a shrug, my skin prickling at talking about this stuff with someone I don't know. "I know what he's going through, the only difference is I know how to control mine."

"Are you sure?" Ri asks as she steps up to me. Her eyes are on mine, like she's trying to read something on my face, or looking for a tell that I might be lying. "You two don't get along and I don't want either of you to lose it."

"I've got him, trust me."

A door bangs and Ri takes off into the corridor, with me and Kane on her heels. Demon comes stomping down the stairs angrily, his face bright red. He's got black cargo pants on with a black t-shirt. A leather jacket too, but the thing that does catch my attention is the straps of leather all over him, filled with weapons, and his hands are covered with black gloves. He walks towards the front door, not bothering to acknowledge either Ri or Kane.

"Cheshire, stop!" Ri demands, her arms folded across her chest. He doesn't falter at her command just keeps on walking like he hasn't heard her. "For fuck sake, Cheshire!"

"You gave me an order so I'm doing what you commanded, Boss," he says, his tone void of emotion, but I hear the sarcasm and so does Ri. I hear her gasp at the word boss, and her hands drop to her sides. There's a slight tremble on her left, and I know she's hurt and trying to hide it.

The door slams behind Demon, and Ri battles to keep her emotions under control with deep breaths. The sound of an engine roars to life outside, the rumble of it almost shaking the foundation of the house. Then it's followed by the screech of tires and I hear the sad sound Ri makes knowing he left.

"What's he driving?" I ask her, but she doesn't acknowledge me. Kane looks at me, his brow lifting, and I can tell from that look alone he's about to ask where I'm going with this. "I need to know what he's driving so I can go help him, I have a certain flair, shall we say, for this sort of stuff."

Ri barks out a laugh, and I smile as she turns to me. "That's a bit of an understatement, don't you think?"

"He will have taken the Camaro," Kane says, and the look on his face tells me he's unsure of what to do now. "Here."

He passes me a piece of paper, and I take it, glancing at the address written on it. I look between them both then nod, grabbing my jacket off the coat rack to my right. Pushing my arms into the cold leather, I grab my helmet and pull the face mask out of it. The material is cold as I pull it over my head so it covers my neck and my nose.

"Really?" Kane asks, and Ri smirks at me. I give her a wink as I pull the helmet on. Trying to hold back the laughter as Kane's eyes widen. "Oh shit," he breathes.

"Now do you see why I said they're the same?" she asks him over her shoulder, and he nods his head. His eyes are still glued to the side of my helmet; I shouldn't have brought this one with me but it was the only one I had in the garage with my spare bike.

"Well, shit!" he laughs, his eyes wide as he looks between the pair of us. "It's about to get interesting."

7

MARCUS

The thump of the bass has me nodding my head along with the music. I don't know what song is playing, but the beat along with the vibrations of the bass in the car are keeping my mind occupied from the voices that have turned up once again. I can't believe they're going to help Reed. Yeah, I get he's called in a favor but fuck! I'm not sure if I can keep myself together long enough for them to get back, Hellion and Rikki are the only things that keep me grounded. Fuck it, I'm going to hurt this fucker, toy with him and drag it out slowly until the voices become a little easier to manage… then I'll follow through and end him.

Hellion's eyes flash in my mind's eye, I can see the hurt there from me being such a dick to her before I left but what was I meant to say? I can't exactly go back and tell her I don't want them to leave.

Shit, man, I've never really had to deal with this shit before. When I did lose it before she and Diamond came along, my brothers left me to it and only came to help if I got myself into a hairy situation. But that was it, I never had to think about how my episodes would affect the people around me. Until Hellion; she helped me in more ways than I could have imagined. She accepted the darkness in me, the fake happy-go-lucky snark I had. She never recoiled from me like everyone does and she's never given me a reason to hate her.

"Damn it!" I roar in the car, my palm hitting the wheel. "Shit. Shit, shit, shit!"

The drive doesn't take long to get to where I need to be, and now I'm here... the darkness swirls within me. It's like it knows what I'm about to do and it's thriving on it, waiting like a wild animal to escape, bringing bloodshed and terror to anyone in its path.

I pull up on the opposite side of the street, my eyes taking in the warehouse in front of me. Flashes of that night filter across my mind's eye; this place reminds me of where shit went down with us and The Grimms. Putting the car in reverse I back up into the alley behind me, shrouding me and the car in darkness. Thank fuck the Camaro is black because, here, it can go unseen it in the darkness. I don't want anyone to know I'm here just yet.

I pull my mask over my face so it covers my mouth and nose, the bottom jaw of the white skull on the front of it is bright against the black material.

I check up and down the street, making sure there's no one around as I hurry across the road to the lone door of the building. My hand grabs the handle and I twist it, testing it, smirking when I hear the click of the mechanism opening.

"Fucking amateurs," I mutter to myself, pulling the door open enough to squeeze through. It swings closed behind me, and I use my back to gently close it so it doesn't alert anyone. Cocking my head to the side, I can hear a raised voice coming from deeper within the building. I listen to see if I can hear any others, but no, there is only one, singular voice.

Silently I work my way through the corridors, keeping my senses alert for any movement. I don't run into anyone... is he here alone? Shit, this guy really doesn't know what the hell he's doing, does he?

"No you fucking idiot!" The nasal voice bellows again. "We both know there are going to be repercussions for the shit I'm doing so, yeah, you need to come and help me."

The huge empty area comes into view and I hold back, keeping my body hidden in the shadows of the corridor. Metal fences surround the room, like makeshift bays for holding stuff. A desk is in the middle, not even twenty feet away from me, gently illuminated by the soft glow of a table lamp. A guy stands there in a crumpled-up white dress-shirt and slacks, pacing back and forth behind the desk.

"No! You listen to me, you said if I helped you with this shit, I would get the town," he growls into the phone; I can't hear the other voice on the end of the line. My curiosity is piqued, wondering if he's the one behind all the shit that's been happening or the one on the phone is. "She's going to come for me, I need you to help me!"

The other person says something, and I'm pretty sure it's not what he wanted to hear if his face draining of color is anything to go by. I notice the slight tremble of his hands, even the one holding the phone trembles against his ear.

"Fuck you!" he bellows.

He must end the call, then he launches the phone. I smirk under my mask, watching and waiting. He's definitely panicking about something, his pacing has picked up and he harshly pushes a hand into his hair, grabbing hold of it. His back is to me as I slink out of my hiding spot, silently. My steps are so quiet he doesn't hear me move into position a foot behind him, but I can hear his muttering, the words are so fast they're inaudible even this close.

"Boo!" He jumps and spins to face me, his eyes widening as he takes me in. The look on his face is pure, unadulterated horror as his head craning back to look up at me.

"I..." he starts but then he goes quiet, his Adam's apple bobbing in his throat as he gulps. I see the tremble of his entire body, and he stands there frozen in place.

"You've been a very naughty boy, haven't you, Ashton?" I ask, folding my arms across my chest, my eyes narrowing on him. He can't see it but I have a huge grin on my face hidden under the mask. The darkness within me swirls harsher than ever, rejoicing at what's about to happen. The blood it craves is the only thing that will sate it now.

"I haven't done anything," he says with a trembling voice, and my eyes don't leave him as I wait for his next move.

"We both know that's not true now, don't we?" I ask, cocking my head to the side. "Why else would I be here?"

"Because your boss is a crazy bitch!" he screams at me, then takes off running in the opposite direction.

My laughter fills the air as I stalk behind him, not bothering to chase him. The sound is menacing even to me, but it feeds his fear enough to make him stumble and lose his balance. He falls to the floor with a thud, his body sprawling out but only for a moment, then he's up, scrambling for purchase on the concrete.

"What you running for, Ashton?" I taunt him as I get closer. "I'm only here to talk."

"Like fuck you are, Southbourne!" he screams as he manages to get his feet under him. "She only sends you when she wants someone dead!"

"Ha!" I bark out a laugh, "We both know, you imbecile, that she's more than capable of ending your pathetic little life all on her own."

"Fuck my life," another voice joins in, stopping us both from saying anything else. My head whips to the left, my eyes narrowing on the shadows at the far side of the room. "Didn't anyone ever tell you not to play with your prey for too long?"

"Who the fuck are you?" Ashton squeaks as he watches the same area I am. She steps into the light looking like a pink-haired angel of death, a mask covering her face which is almost identical to the one I'm wearing.

"What the fuck are you doing here, Pinkie Pie?" I snarl, keeping my attention on the pair of them.

"Boss lady thought you might need a hand." She shrugs as she turns her attention on Ashton. "So you're the one that wants to take it all from The Reaper then?" she says, her tone thick with a drawl. "Wow, disappointing."

"Fuck you, bitch!" Ashton booms, his voice echoing in the empty stone building. He takes off, his arms and legs pumping fast to help him speed up.

"Mine!" Me and Pinkie shout at the same time.

The bitch takes off charging after him with more speed than I thought she would have. Fuck this, my feet thunder against the concrete as my arms and legs pump, picking my speed up. Ashton looks over his shoulder, his eyes widening as he sees the pair of us charging like a set of wild lions after him.

"You can't outrun me, fucker!" Pinkie cackles from a foot in front of me.

My teeth grind together as I push my limbs faster, managing to pass her. I hear her cussing me out as I get to a hair-breadth behind him. I reach my hand forward and the back of his collar is milometers away from the tips of my fingers. Something whizzes past me, making my steps falter and he screams bloody murder. His body bends over and he falls forward, his body rolling across the solid floor.

"Fuck!" he screams as he rolls around, his hands clawing at his back.

"Got ya!" Pinkie cackles behind me, I slow to a stop.

My eyes narrow on the flapping body on the floor, when I see a matte black handle sticking out of his back. My eyes inspect every minor detail of it when realization hits me. It's the same handle as the knife she threw at me back at the house.

"You fucking stabbed me?!" he screeches, still trying his hardest to get the foreign object out of where it's lodged into his shoulder blade. "You crazy bastard!" he screams at me.

"Guilty," Pinkie cackles, saluting him with two fingers, a malicious smile on her face.

"Who're you?!"

I have to admit, seeing him rolling around like this trying to get it out is amusing as fuck. But I've got a job to do, I grip him by the back of his shirt and haul his ass up. Hooking my foot around the leg of a chair close to me, I pull it over and slam him down onto the seat. He screams again as the sudden movement moves the blade.

"Who were you talking to?" I ask, pulling the cable ties out of my pocket and tying his arms to the back of the chair.

"Oh that's kinky," she says with a laugh.

"Shut the fuck up, will you!" I snarl, my eyes jumping to her as I glare. "You're not even supposed to be here."

"Tough shit, they asked me to come," she says with a sarcastic drawl. "So here I am."

Fuck my life, why would they ask her to follow me here? I can't stand her annoying ass, so why? Fuck, how am I supposed to concentrate on what I need to do with her here?

"Fuck off, Pinkie Pie, I don't need any help in making this piggy squeal," I snarl at her, even though my gaze is on Ashton who pales even further at my words.

The leather feels warm against my skin as I pull it off, allowing the cool air in the building to wash over me and putting my sheaths on full display. Each one of them is filled with something, I notice Ashton's eyes bouncing between them and he becomes paler. I never thought that would be possible, but I'm pretty sure he's on the verge of turning transparent.

"So I'll ask you one more time, who were you talking to?" I ask calmly, my tone just as chilly as the air. I drop my leather jacket on the small wooden table with a thick layer of dust covering it.

"Nobody," he says quickly. His tone would sound strong to normal people, but I'm good at hearing what others don't and there was definitely a tremble there.

"I'm not that stupid, Ashton," I sneer, pulling a knife out of the sheath on my rib. "You were arguing with someone on the phone while I was watching you."

My head cocks to the side and I watch his eyes dart all around the room, avoiding me. He even makes the occasional eye contact with Pinkie Pie, who hasn't left like I asked her to. No, she's standing off to my left side, her eyes on him.

"What's a gorgeous thing like you doing here mixed up with the likes of him?" he asks her, his tone all flirty and his eyes running up and down her body. "You are too good for this."

A harsh bark of laughter splits the air, then it turns to a manic sound. The echo of it foreboding as it reverberates around the room. My head whips to her as she loses it, her laughter making her double over, wiping the tears from the corners of her eyes.

"Oh sweetie," she coos, slowly walking towards him, her hips swaying side to side.

This is why I think every woman is a dangerous entity, they

can control a man like this only by a slight movement of their bodies. Ashton is transfixed, lost in the sway of her hips before she stands just to his left, the look on her face sickly sweet as she leads forward. She whispers something to him, and the huge smirk on his face drops instantly. He rears back with enough force to push the chair back onto two legs, tottering there precariously.

"What the fuck did you just say to him?" I snap, angry because I want to know. I hate being left out in the dark and whatever she said has him looking at me with a pleading expression.

"Southbourne," he says, his tone meek as he stares at me. "You do it?"

"What?" I ask with a curious lilt.

"Kill me," he shouts. "Please! I want you to be the one that kills me."

My attention jumps from him to her, he looks to be on the verge of pissing his pants. I notice he's tracking her every movement out of the corner of his eye. She lifts her right hand to closely examine her nails and he flinches at the action.

"Why are you so scared of a little girl?" I ask, flicking the knife into the air with a fluid snap of my wrist. My fingers catch it by the tip, and my eyes are on him rather than the sharpened metal object that could easily slice me with a miscalculation. "She's not the one you need to worry about."

There is a weird sound, and my eyes widen when I realize he fucking scoffed at me, even though I'm the one who is here for him. I'm also the one who tied him to the chair. Yeah, she may have thrown a knife at him, but still.

"Fuck this!" I bellow, losing patience. "Either fuck off, Pinkie Pie, or stay out of my fucking way with this!"

My gaze connects with hers and my top lip curls up just a fraction. She doesn't push me, I'm surprised when she nods her head and backs up a step with her hands up. I turn back to Ashton, my eyes filled with the darkness. I don't know when it happened, but it took over at some point between us chasing him and now. The voices in my head are louder than ever but it feels like my limbs are moving under someone else's control.

"If you're not going to talk, it's time you die."

8

RYAN

The fear on the guy, Ashton's, face is hilarious, but damn the tone that Demon said those words in has a shot of heat going straight between my legs. Am I sick for getting turned on because he said this dude's going to die? Yep, totally! Am I bothered about it? Not at all. I watch with excitement and adrenaline pulsing through my veins as he throws a chain over a metal beam above us, pulling and tugging at it so only a single length of it is left.

The smirk that tips the edges of my lips is malicious, and seeing the way his body moves has another blast of heat hitting. Fuck, it's been a long damn time since I got laid! Ashton gurgles something incoherent as Demon attaches the chain to a collar that's now around his neck. His face is focused as he pulls more chains out of the bag, like he's pulling them out of nowhere. But I'm not stupid, I know he will have had this place scoped out before anything else. That's what I would do, I'm mesmerized as he starts to put more chains in what most people would think is a random placing, but my smile widens as realization dawns.

"Can I help?" I ask eagerly, stepping closer.

He doesn't answer me, his focus is on the task as he secures all the chains in their places. Then he grabs one thick length and my mouth waters as he pulls, hoisting the guy up. The muscles in his back move deliciously under the fabric of his t-shirt.

"I really want to help," I say again.

"This has nothing to do with you, Pinkie," he snarls as he turns to face me. The darkness in his gaze confirms he's on the edge, his once bright eyes are non-existent because his pupils are blown so wide, they swallow the color and the white.

"Ri sent me to help you!" I fire back with a growl of my own. "So let me help."

"Not a fucking chance," he throws back.

I huff, my teeth grinding together and I watch him unwrap all his tools he keeps in a leather wrap. Okay, he wants to be like that, so can I. Walking forward, my steps thudding against the concrete from my boots, I grab the chair Ashton was sitting on and drag it across the floor to where I was standing. Turning it so the back is facing the men, I swing my leg over and settle in to watch how all this plays out.

"You're doing it wrong!" I grind out as I watch Demon torturing the guy. Yeah, he's good with his tools, is he the best? Hmmm I've seen better. No, let's rephrase that, *I* can do so much better.

"Will you shut it!" he snarls, not taking his eyes off the semi-limp guy in front of him.

Ashton looks about a second away from going into the light, the blood loss will be making him delirious but fucking hell, man, I want a go. Is it too much to ask for one teeny tiny little knife to pull some layers off with? It's been too damn long since I've done my job.

"Cheshire?" I whine, should I be embarrassed? Just a little but I don't give a shit, I'm not above playing games like this if it gets me what I want. "I'm bored."

I hear him huff, and my gaze drills into his back. I'm looking for any tell from him that he's starting to thaw towards me, plus, I'm enjoying the view.

Nothing, I get nothing from his body language. My inner petulant child comes out and I start to lean myself forward on the chair, trying to balance it on two legs and not fall flat on my face. I gasp when it tilts forward precariously, and I have to quickly adjust my weight.

"Phew!" I exclaim with a giggle.

"What the fuck are you doing?" he demands, his eyes narrowed on me. I meet his gaze, a massive smile on my face.

"I'm bored," I whine again. "You won't let me play and I've been here, how many days now? I need something to do."

"Well find something then," he retorts. The sound of his teeth gnashing together is violent as he turns back to Ashton's mangled body. "Go back to the house or the club or somewhere as far away from here as you can. I want to concentrate."

"God, you really are an asshole, aren't you?" I mutter with a huff; I don't get him. He seems so happy all the time and the love he has for his Diamond is enough to make any woman melt but then when he's like this, it's like he is four different people at one time. I wonder if his voices are more complex than he lets anyone know?

"Will you—"

"Okay, okay," I say, cutting him off with my hands up in surrender. "Chill, will you, I'll stop annoying the shit out of you if you let me get a closer look at what you're doing."

He seems to think on that, his eyes narrowing as his mouth turns down like he's frowning. I watch, my excitement growing as his face becomes stoic once more. His gaze bores into my own as he gives a swift, curt nod, and I'm on my feet. The chair clatters to the floor as I practically jump over it to get closer.

"You seriously like this sort of stuff?" he asks, his eyes on me.

I nod my head in answer as I look over his handy work, I have to fight to hold back the smirk. Damn, he is good at this, but his cuts and methods are erratic. The edges jagged, looking more like a frenzy than my own smooth edges. My movements are precise, with a reason.

"Why are you cutting like this?" I ask, my tone curious as I continue to examine Ashton. He's still breathing, I can tell from the almost silent breaths he's taking. The sound would be easily missed but I'm tuned in on every little thing surrounding us.

"I want him to hurt but I don't want him to die… yet."

"I get that, but you're too close to a main artery, if you mistake it by a minute amount, he's going to bleed out in seconds." My head cocks to the side as I take in the pale complexion of his toy.

"What would you do?" I whip around to meet his gaze, and he has a blade twirling between his fingers as he stares at me. I search his eyes for any sort of tell he's fucking with me, but I find curiosity shining in the depths.

"Honestly?"

He pulls himself up to his full height and fuck me, I knew he was big but standing next to him now like this, I feel like a tiny little blip. He gives another curt nod followed by a grunt, then he rolls his free hand in a come-on then gesture.

"Honestly, I sometimes like to drag it out but then also I really like hearing people scream when I give them a blood eagle," I say, my tone weird even to my own ears. His eyes widen in shock, and I can't hold back the smirk any longer.

"Seriously?"

"I like to drag it out but, sometimes, I prefer the swift

brutality of it," I say with a shrug. "It all depends on what they've done to get a visit from me, also whatever mood I'm in at the time."

Ashton's breathing is becoming harsher, his chest doesn't seem to be moving. I know he's getting close to falling into the void of death and then he will be no more. Ri is a very clever woman and I know her well enough to know something else has gone on to warrant such a brutal death. It makes me wonder what her other reasons were because if there aren't any and this is the outcome of being a dick and trying to take over, it's a little excessive.

"He's dying," I say, not taking my eyes off the body.

"I know," he replies.

"How're the voices now?" I ask curiously, waiting for the outburst I know is about to come. But it doesn't, I feel him step up to the side of me, our shoulders brushing one another. He doesn't say anything though. Nope, he stands beside me like a damn mountain. "Look, this is the last thing I'll say on it, but I can help you if they get too much. It doesn't make you weak."

A weird sound has me turning my head to look at him, he's staring at Ashton, his face a mask of indifference. You don't have to know this man to know that he doesn't want to talk about it, so I turn my attention back to Ashton as the final bit of his life stutters out. His shallowing breathing stops, his chest doesn't move at all, and that's it. He's had his consequences for thinking he can take something away from the most powerful person in this place.

"You want to get a drink?" I ask.

9

MARCUS

My mind is a mess, as we work fluidly together going through the motions of clearing my stuff away. I've already put a call in to have some of the crew come and take the piece of shit corpse away and clean up. Don't want to be leaving any traces of what's happened here now, do we? Am I worried about it? Nah, the local police don't come to this neck of the woods unless they really have to. I really should head back and start on the rest of the shit that I need to do for Carnal Desires, but I find myself wanting to have a drink with her.

"So, about that drink?" she asks again, her voice doing something weird to my stomach.

"Fuck it," I say, my tone harsher than I wanted but she squeals in excitement, and for the first time, I have to hold back a genuine smile. "Where do you want to go?"

"Not Carnal if that's what you're thinking after the last time we were there," she says with a giggle, and that weird feeling this in my stomach again.

"That's probably a good idea, I don't want to have to pull you down from the pole again," I jibe, and her brows hit her hairline as she mocks horror at me. The smile breaks out across my face and I laugh, and she joins me as we make our way out of the warehouse.

"I'm wondering how you got here?" I ask as we step out into the cold night air.

Damn, I didn't feel it inside but out here it's freezing. I look at her, pulling her jacket tighter around herself as she glances up at me. The coldness and anger I've seen in her eyes since the first day she came isn't there. She smiles at me softly for a second then it morphs into something I can't put my finger on, before we walk across the street to the alley where my car is hidden. My eyes widen as I take in the massive Harley that's on its stand next to my car.

What the fuck?! I'm pretty sure my mouth is on the floor right now as my eyes take in the bike in the dark. I recognize it. Cocking my head, I take it in then turn to her, and it hits me like a fucking Mac truck barreling down a highway.

"Harbinger?" I take a step back, my eyes widening as my gaze jumps between the bike and her. She keeps her gaze firmly on me and takes the step to close the distance I put between us.

"Why'd you step back?" she asks, her tone thick with surprise.

"I…"

How the fuck do I explain to her without sounding like a complete nerd, that I've been dying to meet her. Fuck me, the legends of the Harbinger are notorious in the underground. Everybody, and I mean every-fucking-body, knows who the Harbinger is. Her reputation is one that keeps shitty people doing the right thing. Do I sound like a fucking fan girl? Yeah, I do, because fuck!

"Cheshire?" Her voice is colored with a touch of annoyance as I stand here in shock at the realization.

"Shit!" I exclaim. "Holy fuck, I'm sorry but how the fuck?"

"Let me guess, you thought the Harbinger was a dude like everyone else did?" she asks with a smirk.

My gaze firmly on hers, I give a curt nod. Anyone would come to the same conclusion. The Harbinger has done some diabolical things that have had my stomach churning when I've heard the stories. Words filter through my mind and it's like I've been shocked, my spine snapping straight as I take a step, bringing us closer.

"That's why she told me to ask you?" I enquire, my head cocking to the side as she looks up at me.

"I can see questions burning in your eyes, so how about we go get that drink and we can talk?" She smiles and nods her head back to the vehicles. But I can't move, the smile has me wanting to stay here and keep looking at it, she's so carefree with that look on her face.

"After you."

Pinkie turns and takes the two steps to her bike, then her leg is swung over and the engine roars to life beneath her. I take one big stride and open the car door; the car is low for someone of my height, so I have to make myself smaller to climb in. With one swift turn of the key in the ignition, the engine rumbles. The car and bike make their idling sounds in unison like the beasts are having a conversation that is just their own.

"Follow me," I shout out of the window. I'm surprised she can hear me over the engines, but she nods in acknowledgment, and I put my foot down on the gas and peel out of the alley.

We twist and turn as we drive down the streets, me taking lefts and rights and her following closely. The way she handles that bike, I'll admit that I've been paying more attention to her in the mirrors than I have to the road.

The drive doesn't take long, I pull up fifteen minutes later outside of Sharkie's, a dank bar that's down the street from the pit. I jump out of the Camaro as Pinkie's Harley stops at the side of me. I watch as she pulls the helmet off then yanks down the mask on her face, her smile bright. It slowly drops off as her eyes take in the building and she quirks a brow at me.

"Nice choice," she drawls sarcastically.

I bark out a laugh, turning on my heels and head inside. My veins are buzzing as I walk inside and Aiden smiles at me from behind the bar.

"Fucking hell, how you doing, Marcus?" he shouts down to me from further up.

"I'm good, Aiden," I reply. "You?"

"Yeah, I'm...." His words break off and his eyes widen. "Fuck me! Who's your friend?"

The buzzing in my veins amplified a second ago, I don't need to look to know Pinkie followed me in and she's the one he's looking at like that. The lust rages across his face and a weird tug happens in my gut. He meets my eyes and I shake my head, whatever he sees on my face has him looking back at the glass in his hand as he continues with his job.

"What's your poison?" I say without turning to her.

I hear her chuckle before she steps up to my side, her smell invades my nose and I find myself breathing in deeper to capture it. I've never smelt anything like this before, she smells like fire and blood. But it's intoxicating, I love the smell a fire gives off and the enjoyment I have when someone bleeds, the metallic tang filling the air is enough to make me hard.

"What can I get you both?" Aiden asks as he makes his way down the bar to us. I turn to her, seeing her eyes on the back of the bar.

"Jack and coke," she says, her voice gravellier than I've ever heard it.

My already hard dick thickens to painful levels. Fuck! I'm seriously going to have to get laid, because if this keeps happening every time she speaks, I'm gonna have a real fucking problem on my hands.

"Usual for me," I tell him, turning to lean my back against the bar.

Pinkie does the same and I take in how quiet it is tonight, my brows coming together in a frown. Huh, I know places can have slow nights, but the pit is in full swing tonight and Sharkies is normally heaving when it's going down.

As I take in the bar, I look over her, as she stands next to me and I feel my dick stir, as the scent of her perfume or something wraps around me. I don't get it. Why am I reacting like this to her? I can't stand her ass, but I'm not going to deny she's hot. Like, I would willingly succumb to death by lava just to fuck it kind of hot. My gaze gets drawn to her as she lifts her drink and brings it to her plump lips. The ones that I have thought about being wrapped around my dick a couple of times.

"This way," I say, grabbing my drink from the bar and heading off to one of the booths in the far corner.

Questions have been plaguing my mind for days now and I want to see if she will, willingly, cough up the answers. I know the reason why she's here. To be honest, from what I can gather, her dad is a shitty person. After hearing Hellion talk to Kane about what went down, I'd have done the same thing too.

The leather is worn and cracked as I slide into the booth and Pinkie slides in opposite me. Her eyes are alert, and she seems relaxed-ish, but there is something in her gaze that I take notice of.

"Why were you leaving that night?" I blurt, my outburst has her choking on her drink. Coughing and spluttering as her eyes widen.

"What?" she manages to say between coughs, her breathing faster.

"Why?" I ask again.

"I'm guessing you know everything that brought me here?" she asks, her tone sounding almost nervous. She can't think I'd judge her on something like that, can she? Shit, I'm the last person who could ever judge anyone on anything with the shit I've done.

"I know you stabbed him in the eye," I'm fighting to hold back the smirk as I say it, even a chuckle is building in my throat because I must admit that is one epic fuck you. "I also overheard your reasoning for it, and I don't blame you."

"He's a colossal dick, what can I say?" She shrugs, and I nod in understanding. Yep, I know all about pieces of shit fathers. Look at my own, he was the biggest asshole ever.

"Preach," I smile, then take a mouthful of my drink. Her gaze is firmly on me, it's like she has got me under a microscope trying to read all the little stuff.

"Okay, since you're all about sharing," she jibes with a chuckle. "Tell me who hurt you."

"What?" I ask, confused.

"You were haunted the night at the club so why don't you tell me who it was that hurt you?" she asks, her tone lower.

"No, I wasn't," I fire back, the small sips of the drink I was taking have now turned into me swallowing it in one go. I lift my hand with the glass in it and wiggle it in the air. I know Aiden's seen me as he pours me another.

My skin is prickling and I feel her eyes on me. I want to scratch at my skin to get rid of it, but I know she'll know that the question is affecting me. She's too damn fucking observant for my liking.

"Yeah, you were, so who—"

"Nobody!" I snap, losing my patience. "It was nobody."

"Grow some balls, will you?" she growls, throwing her own drink back. "I told you about him when I didn't really fucking want to."

"Leave—"

"Fuck me, you and Ri are so fucking similar, it's scary," she rumbles, the sound out of place with her features. "She hated talking about anything that hurt her, and you're doing the same thing. Deflecting!"

10

RYAN

Fuck my life! It was hard enough to get Ri to open up when we first met but Demon is as rigid as a fucking wall. I know someone hurt him; it's easily seen in his eyes when a woman tries to flirt with him. He plays it off as being super cool and unaffected, but it makes him nervous, and I want to know why. I have a vague idea, Ri mentioned it when we were talking one night in the early hours without anyone around. She loves him, shit, it's like they're siblings. Yeah, I know they're not related but she told me what he did for her when she was taken. He never gave up hope, and she told me about the other stuff that when down before the whole shit show.

Demon sits frozen in his spot, throwing back drink after drink. His words become slurred the deeper into the drinks he goes. I watch him intently as I get ready to try and haul his ass up and get him to his car. I'm about to tell him enough is enough when he sways sideways. I shoot to my feet, practically diving across the table to grab him before he hits the floor.

"You're really pretty," he slurs, then burps. I can't help it; I smile at him. He giggles like someone has just told a hilarious joke.

"I think it's time to get you home," I say, taking a deep breath. Pulling with everything I have I manage to haul his ass up, I'm sweating like mad, but I do manage to get him on his feet. I hook a foot around the chair and tug it closer and as gently as I can, I help him sit back in it. My phone rings in my pocket, I keep a hand on Demon's shoulder to steady him as I pull it out, my brows scrunching together seeing it's a Facetime from Ri.

"Aiden!" I shout to catch his attention as he's not behind the bar. He comes out of a side door from the far end, his eyes narrowing before they widen. "Keep an eye on him for a second and make sure his ass doesn't fall."

"Okay," he mutters, striding towards me and taking over. Once he's got a hand on Demon and keeping him steady, I rush outside to answer the call. Just as I step out onto the sidewalk in the cool night air, I swipe the call button.

"Fucking hell, it took you long enough to answer," Ri gripes as soon as her picture comes on the screen.

"Yeah, sorry," I say with a quirked brow. "What's up? You can't be missing us all already?" She laughs, like I knew she would, but then her face turns serious. That has my shoulders tensing and my mouth curls down into a frown. "Ri?"

"How did it go with Ashton?" she asks, and I know her well enough that I know she's putting something off. "Everything okay?"

"Why are you deflecting?" I retort. "What's going on?"

"I'm just checking in," she says, her tone sounding like she's miles away.

"Cut the bullshit, Reaper," I snap, losing patience. I didn't realize but I've been pacing the length of Sharkies. I peer through the window and check to make sure Demon is still in his seat, which he is. Thank fuck.

I hear Kane say something in the background, and my teeth

start to grind together the longer she's quiet. I'm just about to snap at her again when I hear a huff and she lifts her eyes to me on the screen.

"I need to call in that favor from you, Harbinger," she says, her face void of any emotions.

It's like someone has just shot ice through my veins at her words, she never ever calls me Harbinger unless something is about to go sideways and she needs the worst thing imaginable.

"What're you needing?" I fire back quickly. "Who for? You're not here so I know it's for someone else."

Kane says something again and I don't catch all the words, but I'm pretty sure he just said, are you sure. If he's worried, then I know it's going to be the kind of thing only I can do. That's why she's not going to ask it of any of his brothers or the crew members.

"I need someone to die," she says, her tone as sharp as ice. The look on her face matches her tone and I feel a small shudder pass down my spine. Because, damn, I know we are both a little on the crazy side, well I'm a lot but I have never seen her use that tone.

"All I'm going to say is it's the one I was telling you about when we were talking," she says, and I feel anger grip hold of me in my stomach. It slowly begins to coil and churn as I wait for her to carry on whatever it is she's going to say. "I need you to go to the pit, now."

My head whips up and I look to my right, the sounds from further down the street suddenly start to echo out of the building. I can hear the spectators screaming for blood and it sounds like a war drum is pounding within the brick walls. My mind races as our conversation flits through my mind, like jagged puzzle pieces with warped edges. Then the night from Carnal Desires comes into my mind, Demon rushing through the club as he looks for someone.

"Get someone from the crew to come and get Marcus from Sharkies and tell Liam I'll be there in a second," I say. I don't bother to wait for an answer, I end the call and spin on my heels, taking the four steps it takes to get to the door of the bar. I pull it open, letting the cold night air in through the gap.

"Aiden, a member will grab Marcus," I shout through the door. "Don't let him leave your sight."

His reply is muffled and the door slams shut. I'm already tucking my hands into the warm leather pockets of my jacket as I walk down the street with determined strides. How fucking stupid is this hoe? My anger builds with every step, the emotions are like a swirling vortex of two dangerous chemical compounds being mixed when they really shouldn't be.

The rumble of a car engine catches my attention, and I slow my strides to a normal pace. The Jeep slows down and the driver looks at me. I realize it's one of the crew members. I've seen him around the house, but I can't remember his name, he gives me a nod and then steps on the gas a little. My gaze follows the car as he drives down the street and pulls up behind my bike and the Camaro. Then he heads inside of the bar, and I turn back to the door of the Pit. There are no signs anywhere, so people don't know what goes on inside. Standing here looking at it you would think it's your everyday abandoned warehouse.

The grey metal door looks bland and kind of blends in with the grey stone walls. My fingers wrap around the cold metal handle, and I push the handle down. The noise it makes grates on my ears, making me wince as it squeaks. The sound from inside that was only just muffled slightly, roars to life without the door in its way. The crowd is going nuts, the beat I heard from Sharkies is the pounding of feet on the bleachers. An incoherent chant can be heard as it joins in with the beat.

My anger swirls more as I walk down the dimly lit corridor. I follow the sounds and make my way deeper into the warehouse, stepping through the thick black curtain at the end. The lights and screams of the crowd roar, grunts and groans coming from within the octagon in the middle of the vast space. Multi-colored lights shoot beams in erratic patterns, swinging in different directions all with the thumping music coming from the DJ booth somewhere in this place.

Two women are going at one another in the cage, their blows are wild and both of them bleed from the open wounds they're covered in. The blonde one seems to be on the last reserves of her energy and the brunette seems to be picking up speed. Her strikes are powerful I'll give her that, but they're not as powerful as they could be with some proper training.

"What're you doing here?" a burly gravel voice says behind me. I look over my shoulder and smirk as Liam steps out of the shadows and towers over me. His huge arms are folded across his chest and he looks down at me.

"Ri sent me," I say, turning back to watch the fight going on.

"What happened?" he demands, stepping to my side, and I feel him tense. "You've got to be shitting me!" he growls. I can feel the anger radiating off him as his eyes lock on to where I'm looking. I know it sounds weird, but I've got an uncanny knack for reading my surroundings.

"That's her then?" I enquire as I turn my head enough to still see him, but also, I'm able to keep an eye on what's going on in the cage if I look out of the corner of my eye.

"This why you're here?" he asks, his tone sounding almost eager.

"Maybe," I reply simply. My eyes are firmly in the direction of everything going on in front of me.

"Yeah, that's her," he growls. "Do me a solid, Ryan?"

"What's that, Frosty?" My interest is piqued. He steps closer to my side, our shoulders brushing as he twists a little at the waist to bring his mouth closer to my ear like he's whispering a secret to me.

"Make it fucking hurt."

The smile that spreads across my face is savage and I turn to face him. By the look in his eyes, he means every fucking word.

"How long's she been here?" I ask, turning my attention back to the cage where the crowd is losing it. Their jeers and whoops ricochet around the building bouncing off the walls, making it build louder.

"Rocco!" he bellows, and I'm surprised when a guy spins in our direction.

He's dressed in a cleanly pressed suit, his hair perfectly styled. He strolls over to us, people moving out of his way as he gets closer. I know who he is after the conversations I've had with Ri, so this is the guy who runs the place when Liam's busy.

"Why the fuck is she in my cage?" Frosty demands, his arms folding across his chest, the action has the massive muscles in there, twisting like a snake under the skin.

"Who?" Rocco asks in a squeaky voice; I have to fight to hold back the smirk as Liam looms over him.

"That,' Frosty growls, his finger pointing to the woman standing in the middle of the cage waiting for the winner to be announced.

"She turned up for the round-robin, Boss," he says, his tone thick with uncertainty. "So, I put her in as one of the women pulled out at the last minute and the cards weren't even."

"Don't you fucking recognize her?" he snarls, his voice sounding deadly. I really wish I had a chair to sit down on and a box of popcorn in my hand to stuff my face with as I watch all this unfold.

From the look on Rocco's face, he hasn't got a clue what

Liam's going on about and Liam himself looks about a second away from boiling a gasket.

"Take a closer look at her, you idiot," he demands, pointing to the brunette one. "Don't you remember the night when Reika came on the cards when she wasn't scheduled to fight?"

The color drains from the dude's face, it's hard to describe but you know when you're waiting for an image to pop up, and that travels down the screen and the colors change before it pops up? Yeah, he looks like that.

"Oh," he says, shuffling from foot to foot. "I…"

"Rocco, is it?" I say as I wave a hand in between the pair of them so they both remember I'm here. "I need you to get rid of the rest of the fighters on the cards and keep her in the cage for me," I say with a sickly-sweet smile. "But if I was you, I would send the other fighters home out of the back door."

"What?" The poor boy looks confused.

"Do as she says," Liam snaps.

Rocco rushes off to do whatever it is he's going to be doing now. Liam turns to me, his face set like stone.

"Can you get the crew here?" I ask as I start to shuffle from foot to foot.

My anger is still there, simmering under the surface but now the thrum of excitement rushes through my veins. The last time I did something like this was when I stabbed my dad. Am I only excited to do this because I get to murder someone? Not entirely, am I this excited to kill this bitch? One thousand percent because I found out she destroyed Demon after cheating on him, he loved her, and Ri did tell me that she broke something within him. I know if she was here, she would rather do it herself but she's off helping Reed so I'm the next best thing.

"Can you do this?" Liam asks, and I lift my eyes to meet his.

I can see the need for revenge on his face, he wants her blood as much as Reika. I don't blame him; Demon is his twin after all.

My smile is demonic as I reach into my pocket and pull the tie out, I quickly pull it over my head. The smile still firmly in its place, he narrows his eyes on me. "Now is not the time for you to tie your fucking hair."

Grabbing a hold of the front of the material I pull it up and settle it into position on my nose. His eyes widen and I chuckle darkly as I pull it off my face.

"Yeah, I'm sure."

"Ladies and gentlemen!" booms through the speaker system. "Can I have your attention, please?" The whole crowd goes deathly silent as Rocco steps into the cage, a massive smile on his face. The crowd leans forward with excitement for his next words. "We've seen this fighter go through round after round, so I'm thinking that we just jump straight to the final match. How about you?"

The crowd goes wild, feet are stamping on the bleachers. The beat echoing like a war drum, *"Yes,"* is chanted louder and louder with each crescendo. They're down for it. I pull a hair tie out of my back pocket and pull my hair up into a high pony.

With a curt nod to Liam, I make my way slowly through the crowd. Guys smile at me, and a few ask me to blow them, I narrow my eyes on each of them. Giving them my meanest stare, with an "*In your dreams*" look.

My leather jacket is warm against my skin, and the crowd is in chaos as the bitch jumps from foot to foot in the center. Her body is littered with wounds from the earlier fights, but she looks like they aren't bothering her at all. I get to the steps of the cage; Rocco's gaze meets mine and I see him pale under the brilliant blue lights overhead.

"Introducing our last fighter of the night," he booms into the microphone. "She's a new fighter to us but trust me she comes highly recommended." He leans closer even though he's nowhere near me. "What do I call you?" he whispers.

"No one," I reply stepping into the octagon.

"We don't know where she comes from or anything else like that. So let me introduce you to the fighter you've all been waiting for… No one!"

The crowd silences for only a few seconds then they explode, jumping to their feet and screaming at the top of their lungs.

"Now, ladies," Rocco says as I step into the middle, facing off with her. "I'd like to go over the rules, the rules are that… there aren't any rules."

My gaze is fixed on the brunette in front of me, she's around my height but smaller than me in build. She doesn't have the muscle mass I have; she looks wiry. Her gaze is on me as she looks me over, her lip curling up in what I'm going to take as disgust.

"Who the fuck are you?" The girl opposite me asks, her tone trying for snarky but it sounds like she's got a bad cold.

"Your reckoning." Her eyes widen in shock as she looks at me.

"I don't know who the hell you are," she throws back.

"Oh, you will."

I lunge for her, gripping hold of her around her throat with my left hand as my right smashes into the side of her cheek. The skin splits like a new cavern being made from the impact. The blood instantly pooling on the surface and carving a path down her cheek as I continue to pound into her face with my fist. Her mouth opens in a silent scream as I tighten my hold around her throat and with a roar, I throw her across the cage. My smile is demonic as she smashes into the metal and hits the mat with a thud.

The darkness within me thrives under my skin, enjoying the bloodlust as I give into the thing I keep a tight noose around to control it. But the thing with control is, yes, it helps ease things in some parts of your life. But every now and then you need to give into your darkest impulses. The blow rocked her, and I watch as she slowly pulls herself to her feet. She's unsteady, swaying just a little. Then she turns to face me, the look in her eyes promises pain and I smile right back in challenge.

"C'mon then?" I call, my eyes seeing past her for a second. The crowd has been vacated from the premises, so it just leaves her and me and a room full of the crew members that she hasn't noticed yet. "Haven't you worked out yet why I'm here, Stacey?" I ask.

"How do you know my name?" she asks, taking her first look around the now empty warehouse. "What the fuck is going on?"

"Were you not told if you came back here, you would pay with your life?" I ask sweetly, walking closer to her. Her eyes are darting everywhere. "Isn't that what you said, Frosty?" I shout.

"Yeah, I did," he says, stepping to the front of the group of crew members. "You should have listened, Stacey."

"I've come back for Marcus!" she screeches. "He's mine."

"Not anymore, he's mine now," I snap, pulling her attention back to me. "Do you really think I'm going to let some hoe like you come back here and try and upset what we have?"

Liam's eyes narrow on me, the look on his face has confusion all over it. The corner of my mouth tips up and I wink. The smile that spreads over his face is savage.

"You've really gone and done it this time, Stacey," he says with a nasty chuckle.

"Marcus loves me!" she screeches.

"No, I don't." My head whips to the right, my eyes widening when I see him standing behind his brother, no emotion on his face as he folds his arms across his chest. His stance is strong, how the fuck did he sober himself up so quickly?

"What?"

11

MARCUS

My top lip curls up in disgust as she just stands there, her eyes wide like she's trying to get a read on me. I fold my arms over my chest, tipping my head up and narrow my gaze on her. Pinkie stands stock still on her side of the cage, her eyes taking me in. Little bolts of electricity flash over my skin making it tingle under her gaze.

"What're you doing?" Liam hisses at me, and I turn my head to look at him. His brow twitches at the stone-cold expression I know is on my face.

A smirk twitches at the corner of my mouth, my arms dropping to my side, and I stride towards the cage not giving my brother a backward glance. The metal steps shake as my boots pound against them, and I have to curl at the waist to be able to fit under the metal padded top of the cage. The opening is small for the average person but for someone of my height and build, it makes it kind of difficult.

"Marcus?" Stacey whines from the far side of the cage, I don't look her way as I take the three steps it takes so I'm standing in front of Pinkie.

Her head tips back so our eyes connect, her brows

scrunching together in a cute little frown as she watches me. I take her in, my gaze sweeping up and down her body. She's still in the jeans and leather jacket she was in at the warehouse. But the difference between then and now is I spot the leather straps crisscrossing across her body that I never noticed before. Sneaky, sneaky.

"What're you doing?" she asks, leaning closer, and her smell fills my nose, the intoxicating scent making me lean forward to be closer to her. *Fuck it.*

A wide smile spreads across my face as she watches me, and my hand lifts slowly. My caress is gentle on the back of her neck. I lunge forward, connecting our lips, at first she doesn't respond to me, her body going still. Then she relaxes just enough, and I pull her flush to my chest, nipping at her bottom lip until she opens for me. I hear the wolf whistles, but they are muted as her lips part and I take that as confirmation she doesn't mind. Our tongues swirl against one another in a sensual dance, and the feel of her has my dick hard as the sweet thing turns darker. The kiss is a battle for dominance as she pushes against me, trying to force me back, our teeth clicking together. I groan, the painful strain of my length against the confines of my jeans is fucking torture.

A high-pitched screech fills the air and Pinkie breaks the kiss, pushing me away from her. The set of her jaw is terrifying as Stacey launches at her, unbridled rage clear on her face. Pinkie's head whips around to look at me, then she winks, a sadistic smirk tipping up the edge of her lips.

I'm going to sound like I've lost my damn mind but fuck me, seeing that smirk as she bounces out of the way of Stacey's blows makes me want to fuck her here and now. I climb out of the cage, even though I don't want to. But I know Hellion has had something to do with this and, honestly, I want to see how it plays out. That bitch fucking broke me when she did what she did, I loved her with all of my being, and then she broke it. I haven't been the same since and when Hellion found out, she lost her shit.

"I thought you couldn't stand her ass?" Liam jokes, coming to stands beside me at the bottom of the steps.

"Doesn't mean I don't want to fuck her," I say with a chuff of laughter. "Plus, are you telling me you don't find the psychos hot?"

"We're all guilty of it, man, look at our dear older brother and his psycho." We both laugh at that, because fuck, could you imagine if shit had well and truly gone sideways between Hellion and Kane? Like fuck, she shot him and was more pissed off that she missed.

A blood-curdling scream fills the air, and both Liam and I look at the cage. Stacey is holding onto the metal fencing with all she is worth, her knuckles brilliant white against the pale skin covering them. Pinkie yanks her feet once, then twice, and rips her off the fencing. Swinging her around with enough force she sails through the air and smashes into the fencing on the opposite side.

"You have a choice," Pinkie's voice is deadly as she stands in the middle of the cage, her arms spread wide. "It can happen slowly, or I can drag it out to really make it hurt for payment of what you put him through."

"Fuck you," Stacey screeches, standing up slowly on shaky legs. "I didn't hurt him."

"Tick-tock," Pinkie taunts her. An evil smile spreads across her face as she pulls something out of one of the holsters.

My heart rate picks up when I recognize the black hilt and the gleaming sliver of the blade. Stacey tries her hardest to back up a step, keeping her eyes on the knife in her opponent's hand.

"Everything that went down between Marcus and I doesn't concern you," she spits at Pinkie, who stands there watching her like an animal working out which part of their prey they want to eat first.

"What's she doing," Liam asks, and I turn to my brother, his face paler than usual.

"What's the one thing Hellion hates doing?" I ask, my voice deeper than usual. The darkness within is precariously dancing on the edge of the surface, it knows there is going to be bloodshed and it's waiting to be a part of it.

He stares off in the way he does when he is really having to use his brain, and I snigger at the imaginary cogs turning in his head.

"She doesn't toy with her opponents, but Pinkie here thrives in it."

Another scream has my head whipping back to the cage, Stacey has a blade buried deep into her shoulder and she's kneeling on the floor trying to pant through the pain. Pinkie has another blade in her hand, twirling it around her fingers. A savage smile creeps up her face as she keeps her eyes on Stacey as she rushes to her feet, lunging forward. Her scream is like a war cry as she wildly throws blow after blow, but Pinkie evades them all too easily. The tinkling giggle falls from her lips as she taunts the other woman. The knife still twirling in her hand, like she isn't moving this way and that to avoid punches. Damn, the control that takes is fucking impressive.

"Stop running and let's do this!" Stacey screeches between pants, her face is now as red as a traffic light. If steam could come out of her ears, I think it would right now. Oh, she is well and truly pissed.

"Who's running?" Pinkie taunts as she spins in a circle. "I'm right here, baby doll, I ain't going anywhere."

"Yeah, you are, and why do you need a blade?" Stacey growls as Pinkie sidesteps her blow again.

"In a fight when someone swings, the other person either

blocks or gets out of the way," Pinkie replies with a sarcastic drawl and shrug. "That's what's happening here, right? We're fighting."

I'm in a weird state of mind as I watch these two, I don't know if it's from boredom or what but fuck my life, can they get to the bleeding portion of this already.

"Hey, Giz." My head whips around to my brother who holds his phone up. I notice Hellion's face on the screen, she's bloody with a cut over her eye. "You okay?"

"Yeah, I'm all good. Has Ryan finished the bitch yet?" she asks, her voice sounding excited.

"Nah, she's toying with her for the shits and giggles. But doesn't help that Marcus decided to play into her lie," Liam cackles as Hellion's brows scrunch together in a frown.

"What're you talking about?" she asks. "Cheshire?"

"Hey, Hellion," I say a little louder so she can hear me, and Liam snorts as he shakes his head.

"What are you doing?" she asks me, but I don't answer. I brush them off because I know if I do answer her, I'm going to get the twenty-one questions about what's going on with me and Pinkie.

"Ryan told Stacey she was with Marcus and my brother decided to throw fuel on the fire by kissing her," Liam laughs harder, and a crew member scoffs.

I whip around to face him, and he pales as my gaze narrows. One of the others pulls him back a step and I lift a brow in challenge. If this little fuck-wit wants to say something he can, but that doesn't mean I'll sit and take whatever shit comes out of his mouth.

"Yeah definitely," Liam cackles, as does Hellion. Turning to my brother I lift a questioning brow which has the pair of them laughing louder.

"Yo, Ryan!" he bellows, catching both women's attention.

"Ri says you should fuck Marcus after this. So, hurry up and do the damn thing, will you?"

Yanking the phone out of his hand, I narrow my gaze at Hellion. She laughs at me as I stare at her, and a heavy booming one joins in with hers, letting me know Kane has been listening to everything too. Manic laughter fills the air, pulling my focus away from Hellion. Pinkie lays on the floor of the cage as Stacey kicks and punches her with everything she has, she doesn't defend herself. But her laughter grows with each blow. Stacey roars as she tries to hurt her but all it's doing is making her opponent laugh harder.

The overhead lights shine on something, causing a blast of light to shine through the room. Stacey screams as she falls to a knee, Pinkie jumps up and slashes with the blade across her back. Then, again and again, carving an erratic picture into her flesh that doesn't make sense. But to me it does, she's toyed with her enough and now she just wants to get this other with.

"Fight me properly," Stacey screams as blood pours down her back.

"Nah, you're boring me now," Pinkie throws back with another slash of the blade across her chest.

The scream is blood-curdling, this cut deeper than the ones on her back. Blood is splattered all over Pinkie's face, and her bright pink hair is spotted with the crimson substance washing out the pink in places. Her eyes are alight as she slashes again, then again. Stacey falls onto her back, screaming from pain and frustration. The roar of the crew is getting louder with every cut of the blade, every person here knows what happened that day. It pains me to know this, but they don't think of me any differently, the one thing we all know is we all can become a product of our environment.

The roar grows even louder, and I take a step bringing me flush to the metal of the cage. My hands grip between the links as Pinkie dives on Stacey. Her body pins her to the floor and she slashes repeatedly like she's possessed while Stacey's scream echoes off the walls. Pinkie continues to cut into her, her victim's blood flying everywhere.

"Holy shit," Liam says from my side. There's a manic look on Pinkie's face as she sits back on Stacey's stomach while the girl lays there, her blood flowing from multiple wounds.

Something flickers against the wall behind the cage, and all eyes turn to it. Ricco stands at Liam's other side with a determined look on his face, his thumbs flying frantically over the screen of the phone in his hand. His fingers are moving with so much speed, the constant click of the touchscreen is making its own music. Everyone hears it since the music was turned off after the last spectator was sent out for this to go down. The flickering on the wall gets worse, then a picture pops up and everyone goes deathly silent.

Hellion snarls something on the massive projection of the Facetime on the wall. "End her miserable existence already."

Stacey manages to make a noise, but it comes out more garbled than anything. Pinkie turns her head back to the woman underneath her, and a shudder rushes down my spine at the set of her face, I feel Liam shudder too. Her top lip curls up in a snarl, then she strikes.

Over and over, she rains down the knife; Stacey's movements were erratic to begin with but as time goes on, they become slower, as do the noises she was making… then there is *nothing*. The whole room is silent, every single man in the building watching as Pinkie remains seated on her victim, her chest rising and falling rapidly, all the while she isn't bothered by Stacey's blood covering her. The effect it has is disturbing on so many levels, well, it would be to normal people.

Slowly, she pushes up off the unmoving body and rises to her feet. The knife in her hand clatters to the mat with a thud, and murmurs break out among the crew. She lifts her head to the ceiling, closing her eyes and opening her arms wide. Her breathing becomes even, the blood still runs down her body, and her face is covered in it, her hair no longer pink in color but a brilliant bright red from the substance.

"What do we do?" one of the younger crew members whispers behind me.

I'm frozen in place, my eyes on the woman who has just butchered the woman I once loved with my whole being. I should be feeling hurt or guilt or something for her being dead, but I don't. I'm *empty,* there's nothing, no swell of emotions. No need to act for revenge, *nothing*. My mind races as I stare at the lifeless body on the mat, memories of that night try to make an appearance and I take a deep breath. The darkness retreats into the deepest recesses of my mind as I breathe easier for the first time since I can remember.

"Your task is complete."

12

RYAN

My body is alive, pulsating and rejoicing with the feeling of ending this bitch's life. Man, this is such a high, killing always brings me joy. I don't know why but being the one to take the life of someone who deserves it, is euphoric. I still remember the first time I took a life; I was eight.

My father had a group of men over to discuss business, so I had to stay out of the way. But I never listened to him, even then, I wanted some cookies. No matter how many times I called through the locked door for someone to bring me something or rang the stupid pull cord for the bell, nobody came. So I climbed out of the window and shimmied my way down the pipe. My heart was racing as I snuck around, slowly cutting my way through the grounds of the compound to the far side of the house where the kitchen was.

The house was quiet, even on the side of the kitchen when I got to the door, or so I thought. A noise caught my attention, and I hid at first, thinking it was one of my father's guards, so I tucked myself into a corner and waited for the inevitable. Then I heard a whimper, followed by a man's voice snapping at someone, telling them to shut up, I've always been curious. I had seen way more than any child should have so I stepped out of my hiding spot and peeked my head around the door of the kitchen.

Sasha, one of the kitchen staff, was on the floor, huddled up; her hands over her head as a man kicked and punched her. She was so scared, tears streaming down her face as he continued to beat her. His words still echo in my mind every now and then to this day, *"Nobody will believe you; I'll tell them you were asking for it, slut."*

I didn't know what he meant by that until later on in life when I saw first-hand the atrocities people are capable of. But seeing her so scared and begging him to leave her alone, made me angry. My mother used to be the same with my father, pain always surrounded him. Sasha saw me and she tried to wave me off with a hand, but the man noticed. His accent was weird to me, I'd never heard it before. Then the next thing I know a hand reached for me from behind the door, grabbing me around the neck and pulling me into the kitchen. Sasha screamed, her feet slipping on the floor as she scrambled to get up.

"*Leave her alone,*" she shouted at the man, but he just laughed, shaking me in his grasp.

My scream filled the air as I did what my mom taught me, she always said *if someone is hurting you, do whatever you can to get away.* So, I pulled the last gift she gave me out of the pocket of my jeans and stabbed him in the neck with it. His scream of rage still plays in my mind, the image of standing above him as the light went out in his eyes.

"Pinkie?" I shake my head, pulling myself out of the memory. My lids flutter as the lights from the pit come into view, Demon standing in front of me with worry etched all over his face. "Are you okay?"

"Yeah," I croak, my voice sounding like a starved man who has gone months without water. I try to gather salvia in my mouth to help quench the dryness but it's as if all the liquid within me has vacated the premises.

The room is deathly silent as I look around. The crew members that were here all stare at me with wide eyes. Some of them look to be on the verge of throwing up and I have to snigger at that, they're a part of the Reaper's crew and the sight of a little blood has them wanting to hurl. My eyes get drawn to the ground, and there she lays, her eyes wide in horror for the final moments of her life.

"Take it I zoned out?" I ask, lifting my head to look at Demon. He's so damn close our chests are brushing one another with each breath either of us takes.

"Where did you go?" he asks, his voice low; I smile at him. There's no need for him to try and keep our words quiet as there is no one close enough to hear.

"No doubt the same place you go," I reply with another smile.

He tenses at my words; his eyes widen for a second before his brows scrunch together into a frown. My head drops to the side as he stands there, stock still, the frown still on his face from my words. I lift my right hand and smooth the lines on his forehead with my thumb and he relaxes at the touch, his eyes widening again.

"Hey." The word has me looking behind him at his brother, Liam, who stands there shuffling from foot to foot like he's intruding on something. "You can't go out like that, there's a shower in my office you can use, and take any of the spare clothes."

"Thanks," I say as I brush past Demon who is still frozen in place.

The gathered crew members part like the Red Sea as I walk through them to the door that leads to the office. Just before I step through, I look over my shoulder and see both brothers deep in conversation, Demon's eyes are on me. I wink and then step through into the long corridor that has the office on the end. I find a box to the left of the door with the words spare scrawled across the side of it. Pulling the top open I'm surprised to find some black sweats and a hoodie on top that look like they will fit.

A towel hangs on a hook above it, so I pull it off and throw it over my shoulder as I head to the only door in this room. The door squeaks swinging into the bathroom with bright white tiles along with the white fixtures. I hit the switch, and a brilliant yellow light fills the room, huh, so maybe it's not that bright in here after all. My eyes span the room and I notice the small window on the right, even though it isn't the size of a normal window. The moonlight overhead shines bright out in the darkened alley. I would probably struggle to squeeze out of there if I had to.

The shower is a decent size for a place like this. I turn the handle and the water springs to life out of the massive head. I smile when the water runs out of the waterfall head; that is the one thing I miss from the compound, my shower. I would spend way too long in there, but it had a waterfall head too, with jets on the bottom that helped ease my aching muscles. I place the sweats and hoodie down on the side and hang the towel on the hook on the outside of the shower screen.

My brow furrows as I peel the jacket off my shoulders and then take hold of my top. Pulling it up, it peels away from my skin with more effort than is usually needed. My eyes drop to my stomach, and I see dried blood sticking everything to my skin. With a harsher tug, the top comes over my head and I drop it to the floor. It's a bloody pile on the floor as my bra adds to it. I make quick work of stripping myself of the clothes with her blood on and steam begins to fill the room.

Looks like I'm going to have to burn my shit, fuck, I really fucking liked that jacket too. The thought has a growl passing my lips, "*Ugh, next time remember to take your favorite stuff off before you carve someone up, you dick!*" I mentally chastise myself.

Thank God for Liam and him spending so much time here, some of Ri's things have been left here too. I guess, it makes sense that the feminine shower gel and hair products are hers unless Liam has more women passing through this shower than any of us know. Hmmm, that's a thought and maybe not too far from the truth as he never brings a woman to the compound, from what I've heard the crew talking.

A noise catches my attention and my head tilts to the side as I continue to scrub the blood harshly off my skin. My attention is focused on listening for another sound, and I swear if some fucker is in here; I'm going to be seriously pissed the fuck off. Can't a girl shower in peace? Something squeaks again and I put the loafer back on the shelf in the corner of the cubicle and raise my hands into a fighting stance. I slow my breathing, even though my heart rate has picked up and now thumps erratically in my chest.

A shadow shines from the light, the figure stretching up the shower curtain. My hands are steady in the guard I put them in, and I watch whoever it is stalk closer. Bouncing on the balls of my feet just a touch, I prepare to dive out of this thing and fuck up whoever was stupid enough to come in here. The shower curtain rips back, and I swing.

"What the fuck?! Cheshire!" I bellow as he stumbles back a step from the punch I just hit him with. "Why are you in here?"

He straightens himself up, his eyes are dark as he wipes the blood from the corner of his mouth. His eyes track up and down the length of my body, widening a fraction, but then his eyes meet mine. I fold my arms over my chest and glare at him as the water continues to beat down the side of my body.

"Why?" His tone is more gravelly than I have ever heard it and my brow quirks up as I cock my head to the side, taking in the sight of him. I know what he's asking, he wants to know why I killed her.

"Get out," I say as I unfold my arms, then pick up the loafer and start to wash myself once again.

"Answer me," he demands.

"I'm not talking to you while I'm in the damn shower, dude, so get the fuck out and wait in the office!"

The water is heavenly as the hot goodness hits my skin and I close my eyes, soaking in the feeling, my muscles relaxing. I don't hear anything; no words are spoken, and I can't hear him breathing so he must have done as I asked and gone to wait in the...

My back slams against the porcelain tiles and I growl. My vision settles from the movement to find Cheshire standing nose to nose with me, his dark eyes narrowed as the water beats down on us, soaking his hair and clothes.

"Why?" he asks again.

My palms land on his shoulders and I push at them, my chest rising and falling rapidly as I heave with everything I have. He doesn't move, only presses himself closer. My eyes widen as I take in the wildness in his eyes, the darkness I have seen so many times is driving him now, he is well and truly lost in the void.

"Cheshire?" I say softly, trying to coax him out of it enough. "I know it's riding you hard, dude, but you need to back up."

"I need you to answer the fucking question, Pinkie," he snarls, his fingers wrapping around my neck as he pushes my head back against the wall. Titling my head up, I meet his eyes fully.

"If I answer, will you get out of the shower?" My voice is

strong, but I've seen this many a time with myself when I've gone too far; Damn, he's in worse shape than I first thought.

He gives a sharp nod, then his eyes run down the length of me once more, slowly tracking a path down over my breasts towards my toes. His eyes stay there for a second before slowly working their way back up to meet my eyes and a tremble washes over me, not because of fear; No, it's not that, he's the first person I've met that I can connect with on more than one level.

"Ri asked me to end her life if she ever came back," I say, letting my body relax against the wall. I can tell he doesn't want to hurt me; he just wants answers for what went on in the cage. "But honestly, she told me what went on with the pair of you and I would have done it even if she didn't ask me to."

"Why?" he growls out again.

"Because when you love someone as much as you loved her and she was meant to love you; Nobody, and I mean nobody deserves to be shit on the way she did you." My tone is softer, almost meek as memories of my own betrayal flash across my mind. But the difference between his and mine is, he only saw her cheating on him.

My eyes shoot open as a feeling of something like a soft caress brushes against my cheek, and my eyes lock with his gaze. The dark pools that were there have softened enough to show me the guy hiding underneath. He watches me as the water continues to beat down on him. Being out of the path of the water; I feel the cold early morning air and I tremble from the effect of it. He steps back, pulling me into the path of the scorching hot water, so it hits both of us.

"I answered your question, can I finish my shower now?" I ask with a smirk.

He cocks his head to the side, like a cute puppy does. I gasp when his mouth connects with mine; One of his hands twines into the hair at the back of my neck as he pulls me closer to him. Even though it's not possible, he still tries to get us closer. Our tongues twist and turn against one another and I kiss him back with as much heat as he kisses me.

My head is spinning as he deepens the kiss, the pressure becoming more intense and my back presses harshly against the tiles once again. The pleasure from the pain is glorious as I claw at his shoulders trying to fuse our bodies together. He smiles just a little, the corner of his mouth tipping up by a fraction, but he doesn't break the connection between our lips.

A need I haven't felt in a very long time consumes me as I lower my right hand, the palm running down his stomach toward the top of his jeans. My fingers dip into the top of the fabric, and I feel blazing hot skin. I manage to break our connection, turning my head to the right out of his path. But that doesn't stop him or his lips from leaving a wet trail as they carve a path down the side of my neck to where my shoulder meets it.

"We have to stop," I manage to get out between my panting breaths. I gasp as his fingers tighten just a touch around my neck. The move forces me up onto my tip toes, and he pulls back enough to look me in the eyes.

"Why?" he asks gutturally.

"Cheshire," I say softly, taking his face in my hands. "You don't like me like that."

Wow! Look at me being all responsible and shit; But I can't let this continue, even though I want to. I don't want him to regret it and feel guilty afterwards, because I know he will. He'll feel like he took advantage of the situation and knowing him as I do, it will eat him up inside.

"How do you know?" he growls, pushing a denim-clad thigh between my legs. I slam my lips together, sucking them into my mouth to hold back the moan that's in the back of my throat. The material on his thigh rubs against my clit again, and I feel my whole body tremble once more.

My head is spinning as he rubs my clit over and over with the denim, a smirk on his lips as he watches my face intently. The zing of electricity that pulsates through my body from that one small movement has me pushing my chest forward to bring myself closer to him. He smiles wider at this; and my mouth becomes dry as I try to gain control over my wayward libido.

"Ryan?" he says, his voice thickly laced with lust, the baritone rumbling in the back of his throat and my already dry mouth turns into the Sahara Desert. "I like to fuck a lot, and so do you." He smirks. "How about we just let this happen, no emotions, no expectations of anything and we can go back to hating each other tomorrow?"

The sensations are too much, I close my eyes and his words play on repeat in my head. I haven't been laid in such a long time, why not? He continues to tease my sensitive spot, my head becoming even more fuzzy from the feelings growing low in my stomach. Fuck! I want to come so bad…

"What do you say?" he rumbles, pressing harder on my sweet spot.

My breaths become shorter as the feelings low in my core continue to escalate, I lunge forward, fusing my lips with his. His growled response has another moan building in the back of my throat. Our tongues twist and swirl as the kiss builds in fever, and my body starts to heat. That was all the conformation he needed, he growls from the back of his throat and pushes me into the tiles.

My lust builds, and the sane part of my brain is telling me I need to stop this, but I've gone too far now to be able to rein myself in. I claw at the soaked t-shirt at his back, grabbing a fist full of the material and tug, but I'm met with resistance. My snarl of frustration echoes around the cubicle, and Marcus laughs as he lets go of me. Without moving his thigh he pulls back, his eyes dark with lust. He grips his t-shirt at its bottom and rips it over his head with more ease than I managed.

My eyes widen as I take in the tattoos covering his chest and torso, they all look like intricate details that bring forward a massive picture. There are skulls with lettering in an old style of writing that makes it hard to read, then there is some weird circle thing I can see the edge of on his left bicep. The whole picture looks like what he feels like living in the darkness that haunts him. I feel a tug in my chest as I resonate with the feeling and the look of the tattoo because that's what it is like living in my own void.

I lift my hand to trace the lines, following them as they twist and turn across his chest and drawing a line down over his abdomen. He sucks in a breath from the featherlight touch, and at the movement, I lift my eyes to meet his.

"I know these feelings well," I say, tracing the figure of a grey person, or shadow-type figure, that stands in the middle with their head raised, and I know that they're screaming for help.

His lips crash down on mine, our mouths starting the lust-filled dance. But I don't move my hand, I lift it to his heart and keep it there as my thumb rubs gently back and forth. She isn't the only thing that made him this way and, shit, for an image as painful as that... what the hell has he been through?

His hands move to the button on his jeans, my eyes following the movement and breaking the connection between us. Anger and lust roll off him in waves and I know that my mentioning the images on his chest has pissed him off for some reason. He isn't a big talker about his emotions, that much I can tell. But still, he can't think it's possible for him to keep everything to himself without getting to a point where he explodes because something triggers him. I chew on the inside of my cheek, at war with myself as to whether I should say something to try and lessen his anger, but then there is a chance I can make it worse.

He growls, the sound so much like a caged animal and it has my head whipping up to look at his face. His brows are scrunched together, and the rest of his face is twisted up into something demonic-looking. He yanks at the jeans again, his frustration growing, I yelp in surprise as he grips hold of my shoulder hard and spins me around, pushing my face against the tiles. The hard surface pushes painfully onto my cheek and my bone feels like it's about to snap under the pressure. I try to push myself back, but I can't, he's using every ounce of strength he has to keep me here.

"Marcu—"

I cry out as pain rips its way through me, the intrusion is excruciating as tears fall from the corners of my eyes. The feeling of being ripped in two roars through me as he forces himself the rest of the way into me. He leans forward, panting against my back, but my mind flickers to the pain and back to him sprawled against my back. The tears fall freely, the water from my soaked hair helping to hide them, and a metallic tang rapidly fills my mouth as I try to breathe through the pain. My mind can't fathom why he would do this, it's like trying to fit something into the head of a bottle but when you realize it won't fit, you force it anyway, no matter the consequences.

The pain and shock start to dwindle as I become accustomed to his size because, fuck me, he is packing some serious equipment. I don't know if I should be spitting venom, pissed he did that without any warning or if I want to carry on this with a carnal fuck.

"Shit!" he hisses, and the weight of him lifts from my back. "Tell me you're okay?"

"That's an asshole thing to do, shithead," I snap as I use my right hand to wipe the tears of pain off my face. "No serious foreplay and you decide to slam home."

"I…"

My muscles relax enough to enjoy the feeling of him. I take a deep breath and pull my hips towards the wall. I only manage to move them maybe an inch or two but it's enough for my eyes to roll at the sensation of him moving out of me. I hear him hiss in surprise as I push myself back down on his length, a groan escaping me as my walls fight to keep him fully seated.

"Ryan?" he says in almost a whisper as he leans over my back, bringing his mouth to my ear. "I got carried away, I'm so sorry."

My limbs lock in surprise at him saying sorry so sincerely, my mind can't wrap around the way he said it for the man I know him to be. But he doesn't need to say sorry, I get it; I really fucking do, but shit, man.

"Don't get all soft on me now," I gripe as I move my hips again, it's not enough this time to give me the sensation I'm after with his huge heavy frame limiting my motion. "It happened but, dude, if you don't start fucking me in the next second, I will rip your dick off and do it myself!"

A bark of laughter fills the air, but the sound is mixed with surprise. The next instant, his weight is gone from my back and he pulls out of me enough so only the tip of him is still inside. I push back on my arms so my face isn't against the tile. He slams into me and I moan as I drop my forearms on the wall to stop my face from smashing into it again. My hair moves and I feel him twine it around his hand as he yanks my head back to a painful angle and pounds into me. The sounds of our joined moans filling the air over the beating of the shower has my head swirling like there is a tornado inside it. The sensations crashes over me in waves, once, twice, three times.

"Fuck, you feel so fucking good," he groans as his hips pick up to a punishing pace, and all I can do is grit my teeth, losing myself in the feeling of being owed and fucked so thoroughly that my voice has left the building and the only sound I can make is another moan.

Everything I'm feeling coils and pulses low in my stomach as I writhe and moan, my ass pushing back against him with each thrust of his hips. The action has his already brutal pace becoming so much more than I thought could be possible.

"Cheshire," I pant. "Please, I need to come."

"Not yet," he rumbles, the baritone sounding like it's come from somewhere deep in his chest. This has another round of lust flooding my system and I moan louder, the sound echoing off the walls. My hair lands on my back with a thump from all the water in the strands, and my muscles relax at not being pulled so taut. The break lasts not even a second as his hand wraps around my throat and squeezes once before he pulls me back. The back of my head rests between his chest and shoulder, and his hold tightens again as the new angle changes the sensation for the pair of us.

"Please," I beg for the first time in my life.

He doesn't answer, his free hand working torturously around under my boobs, the feather-light touch has a shiver washing over me like a tsunami, but he doesn't stop fucking me like a man possessed. He trails his fingers down a line from my sternum towards my bellybutton and then keeps going.

My nails feel like they could snap with the amount of pressure I'm pushing them into the wall with, my hands trying to grip onto something for all its worth but I can't. My whole body is shaking violently, the only thing keeping me on my feet is the hold he has on me.

"Now!" he growls out, his command washing over me is too much.

I scream as my orgasm explodes, wave after wave it rolls

over me but he doesn't stop, turning one into two. Tears stream down my face, my vision is blurry as dark spots dance at the edges of it, threatening to pull me into the darkness. I pant, trying to help myself through the onslaught; then the room spins.

I yelp as my knees slam into something, and a shadow looms in front of me—I think, I can't tell much with my blurred vision. My head is pulled back at a painful angle and the blurriness clears enough to see Demon looking down on me with a feral expression.

"Open your mouth."

My brain follows the command, my mouth opening as I still try to concentrate from being so thoroughly fucked. Thick white jets of cum hit my face and tongue as he throws his head back and moans his own release and I act on instinct, wanting to give him something like he just has me. So I take my thumb and wipe his release from my cheeks onto my tongue and swallow. His eyes heat once again at the action and I can't fight back the smirk.

"Shit!" Our heads whip to the right and I freeze, spotting a surprised Liam standing there with the shower curtain in his grasp. "Marcus, I need to talk to you."

13

MARCUS

My asshole of a brother just stands there with a big shit-eating grin on his face, his eyes jumping between mine and Pinkie's. My eyes drop to her and she's frozen on her knees, just staring at him. I smirk seeing the pissed-off twist to her mouth, and I hold back a laugh because she looks to like she's about to chew his ass out.

"Get out," I growl at him, much to his amusement. But he doesn't leave, he just stands there with that stupid look. "Liam."

He raises his hands and backs away slowly. His eyes drop to Pinkie again and he winks, then chuckles when I growl at him. I know him well enough to know he's planning on saying something to piss me off.

I gently unwrap my hand from her hair, my eyes dropping to her as I feel her shiver at the touch. She's glaring at me now, and the anger I see shining in the depths of her eyes is hot as fuck. I open my mouth to say something, but close it again because what the fuck do you say to someone after fucking in a shower?

With a growl, she pushes herself up until she's standing but I spot the tremble in her knees as she stands in front of me with a raised brow. I grab my t-shirt off the shower floor but then drop it because it is soaked. I look at Pinkie again and she's still standing there, looking steadier on her feet now, but her brow is still lifted.

"I..." I start to say but then shut up, I give a swift nod and step out of the shower. The cold air instantly washes over me the further to the office door I get away from the steam.

Liam is leaning against his desk with a massive grin on his face when he spots me in the doorway. I'm frozen in place, the urge to turn and say something to her making me fist my hands trying to decide what I would say.

"Close the door, will you?" she says, which unfreezes me, my eyes widening a touch at the tone. It isn't pissed off but it did sound annoyed. Taking hold of the door handle I swing it closed and step out into the office.

"Have fun, did you?" Liam jests.

"Shut it," I snap, not wanting to deal with his shit now. The darkness is back with a vengeance and a moment of panic sets in. Shit, my pills are back at the house. "What's up?"

"There's some shit going down on the southside, apparently a group is causing some shit saying they're taking over," he says with a faraway look on his face.

"Okay, so why come to me?" I ask curiously.

"Well after seeing that, I thought you might have wanted to blow off some steam," he snickers. "But I see you made better use of your time."

"Don't," I growl out in warning.

"Was she any good?" he asks, sitting straighter. It's almost like he's leaning forward waiting for the gossip like an excited schoolgirl.

I round on him, and his eyes widen as I take a step closer.

"Chill." He chuckles but I hear the tremor in his voice. "Shit, I was just joking with you."

Turning my back on him, I walk over to the only other door in here, grabbing a t-shirt and sweats from one of the shelves. Pulling the dry t-shirt over my head in a quick motion, I shove my soaked jeans down to my feet and step out of them, then slip the sweats on. The cold isn't as bad now as a second ago while wearing wet clothes.

"Is that all the info you—"

The door to the bathroom opens and a fully clothed Pinkie steps out. My mouth waters and my eyes scan the length of her body. She's raided the spare clothes and I can tell it's Hellion's stuff but fuck me, she doesn't half know how to fill out sweats.

"Enjoy your shower?" Liam snarks. I look over my shoulder to him and give him a warning glare that he chuckles at.

"Wow, you're that shocked you walked in to see me swallowing your brother's cum?" she sasses. "What's so surprising? He's hot." I bark out a laugh at her admitting I'm hot, she doesn't look at me though. "Or is it because you wished it was you?"

He doesn't say anything, just glares at her and the thoughts in slam into me. Does he? Rage rolls through me as I turn to look at my brother, and I see the ashen expression on his face as he looks at me.

"Bro?" he says.

Tinkling laughter fills the air as I murder my brother where he stands in my head, and I'm pretty sure my expression tells him exactly what I'm thinking.

"I'm going to bed, have a nice day, boys."

My eyes follow her as she heads out of the office without a backward glance, even when she's no longer in the corridor my eyes stay glued to where she was. The darkness demands I follow her and fuck her senseless again, and the realization has me rubbing my fingers against my temples.

"Are they back?" the words are snarled, and I know he saw

it. I turn to face my twin and he's standing there with a pissed-off expression, his arms folded across his chest. It's a typical Liam stance that all the crew except me, Kane, or Hellion are terrified of. I lift a brow in a challenge and cock my head, watching him.

"Dammit, Marcus, why the fuck haven't you told anyone?" he demands, stepping closer to me. He's dropped his arm but then he grabs a hold of the back of my neck and pulls me forward until we're nose to nose. "You promised that you'd say something, I'm not losing you like last time."

"I'm fine."

"Cut the bullshit!" he roars in my face.

With everything I have, I shove him off me, satisfied when he stumbles back, his eyes narrowed. I turn my back on him and head to the door, I need to get some sleep beforehand.

"I've got it handled, brother," I say before stepping out of the office and shutting the door while he charges after me.

My stride quickens, eating up the ground when I hear the office door fly open and crash into the wall. He's going to do one of two things; one, he's going to chase after me and carry on pushing even though I've answered him or, two, he's...

My phone vibrates in the pocket of my sweats, the fucker. He went with option two. I pull the phone out and sure as dammit, Hellion's name flashes across the screen. I watch it for a second and it rings off, but then it starts ringing again. I hit the end call button and stuff it back in the pocket of my sweats. Rocco shouts at me from the other side of the warehouse and I glare at him, he doesn't try to come over so I head out front.

The sun is blinding as I pull up outside the house, when I get outside Sharkies, Pinkie's bike isn't there but the trash can has dying embers from a fire. She's good, I'll give her that, she burnt her shit but didn't bring it to the house so she clearly knows the cameras surrounding the bar are fakes. They were put there to deter idiots from starting shit and, for the most part, they do. But then her knowing leaves me with one question, how long has she been here before showing herself?

The drive back was a strange one, my thoughts kept turning to her. My dick hard, instantly remembering the way she felt under my hands and, fuck me, the way she swallowed my cum was, mmmm. Turning the car off I sit on the drive, my eyes scanning the house as I sit here and compose myself. Was she pissed at me? Did I hurt her? Shit!

Decision made, I throw the door open, the gravel crunching under my boots as I climb out of the car. The house is quiet, no doubt some people are still asleep but if what Liam says is true, I bet some of the members are out pounding the streets to see what they can pull up about the newcomers. My steps eat up the ground as I make it across the garden and throw the door open, taking the steps two at a time. I'm outside her door, my hand raising to knock but, for some reason, I can't bring myself to do it.

But I can't leave either, it's like my feet are frozen in place as I battle with myself. But then I remember our conversation from this morning.

"No feelings, and no expectations."

14

RYAN

My head is a mess.

I'm sure I heard someone outside my door earlier. I could have been imagining it, but if I didn't, why would they be there unless it was Demon? Although, we did agree on the simplest thing. The agreement serves me just fine because it will be a matter of time before I decide to move on, either of my own free will or if I'm forced to. I really don't think my father would come here though because if he was going to, he would have shown up by now. *Fuck,* what is wrong with me? I'm overthinking everything.

Dammit! Jumping up off the bed, I grab some clothes from the top of the dresser and head into the bathroom. After a quick pee and cleaning my teeth, I flip the shower and wait for the steam to fill the room. I step in and hiss instantly as the scorching hot water hits my side, the temperature so hot it feels like it's trying to flay my skin from my body. I make quick work of washing, my veins are buzzing and I need to get out of here for a bit. My body is dry and fully clothed in what must be record time, and my hair is towel dried—but I'm not out to impress anyone so fuck it. Tying it in a messy bun on top of my head, I head to the door.

My eyes scan the corridor and I internally slap myself, what does it matter if I come face to face with him, for fuck sake, we are both adults. Now Liam is going to be another issue, he had way too much fun last night being a dick. But then again, if he starts shit once more with me I'm not opposed to wiping the grin off his face with a beating. My phone starts vibrating in my pocket, I pull it out finding Ri's name flashing on the screen.

"Hey, you okay?" I ask, a little too eager, but I'm kind of hoping she's ringing to ask for some help with whatever it is she's doing.

"What the fuck went on last night?" she demands in her big boss-woman tone.

"What?" I ask, playing dumb. "Ri, I haven't got a clue what you're going on about."

"Fuck off, Ryan, I don't give a shit that you and Cheshire were fucking, I want to know why you haven't said anything about him losing himself in his voices," she rumbles, the sound would be terrifying to anyone else hearing it but I know she's panicking about him.

"What?" I ask, my mind starts reeling as I try to remember if I saw any hint of the darkness within him last night but he seemed perfectly fine, he was rough so that could have been a sign but I can handle it. "Yeah we did fuck, but, Ri, I didn't see any sign he was losing it."

"Really?" she sounds stunned. "Liam rang last night saying he's really worried about him."

"I don't know what to tell you, Ri. He seems fine to me."

The look on her face has me, sitting up straighter. "Ry, I can understand why Liam was so worried, he looked like he was going to lose it when I was in the cage, but after. He was fine, unless Liam was worried about the joke I made about him wishes it was him, that pissed Marcus off. But that was quickly forgotten."

"So Liam walked in on you both?" she teases.

"Yeah, not a chance, bye."

I end the call but not before I could hear her laughing down the line. *Bitch*! She going to be an asshole about me and him when she gets back. But I'll be the first to admit to myself that the guy knows how to fuck, like seriously, I've never had an orgasm hit me so damn hard I nearly passed out from it. Lust slams into me just from thinking about this morning, and I grit my teeth until the sensation passes. Okay, note to self, don't think about it unless I want to fuck, got it.

My veins begin to buzz, the lust still rolling through my body. Yeah, I definitely need a damn drink. Lifting my head high, I step out into the open. Fuck it, if I bump into any of them I'm a grown-ass woman and I can deal with the gossip.

It's strange as I walk through the house, there isn't anyone around. Huh, I pull my phone out and look at the time. Okay, now that makes sense, it's nearly eight at night. Damn, I slept the whole day away, who knew?

I make it out of the house, but it's a little unsettling even for me. The garden is quiet, I wonder what's going on. My steps are long as I stride over to my bike, picking my helmet up and putting it on as I swing my leg over. The engine rumbles to life between my legs and I can't help the smile that spreads across my face. Yeah, I know I look like a mad woman but I have to snigger because I remember when I first got it and some sexist prick asked me if I bought it to make myself come. I laughed at the snide comment, which he took as an invitation to get closer to me, then I smacked him in the mouth and pissed myself laughing as his lip and nose exploded.

The gravel kicks out behind the bike as I take off with a screech of rubber. Fuck it! I'm going to check out The Den, Ri said it would be somewhere I would like to hang out and maybe I can get to meet her cousin Paine. I haven't seen him since I got here and I'm curious about her lost family member.

The streets are winding down from the heavy traffic, plus, to be fair, there's no issue with traffic around the area The Den is located. The roar of people laughing and joking hits me as I round the corner, my eyes widening when I see the crowd that's already waiting in line to get in. Seriously, I've never seen a queue go all the way down the block and disappear around the corner. Pulling into the alley at the side, I make sure my helmet is secured to the handlebar, then head around the corner. The guy on the door nods at me as soon as he sees me and opens the door.

"Hey, do you know if Paine's in?" I ask as I get to the side of him.

"Boss-man is behind the bar," he grunts as he turns back to watch the waiting crowd.

The corner of my mouth twitches at being dismissed by the brute with a finality that makes me think he and I would get along swimmingly. The corridor leading into the bar isn't as long as I thought it would be. I at least thought it would match the one going into The Pit but, nope, I barely blink and I'm stepping through, my mouth dropping open as the heavy beat of the music vibrates under my feet.

Damn, Ri wasn't joking. Excitement bubbles up inside me like a toddler being let loose in the candy store. Holy shit, everything is neon and the bar at the back looks so fucking fancy. Ri said when she gave control to Paine he asked if he was okay to remodel it, but now I really want to know what it looked like before. My eyes get drawn to the massive bar again, the bottom half of it looks like lava is flowing out of thin air and then it disappears into the floor.

"I take it you must be Ryan?" I spin to the voice that is way too close to be able to speak into my ear and be easily heard over the music.

On instinct, I step into a guard position, ready to attack first if I need to and a deep chuckle has me cocking my head as a guy steps out of the shadows. Holy shit! This guy is massive, easily as big as Reapers boys and, from what I can only gather, is covered from the neck down in tattoos. My brow quirks as he smiles so wide he shows brilliant white teeth against the olive tone of his face. His glare seem to glow under the lights, bleaching both his eyes and hair of any distinguishable coloring as his hair flops into his line of vision.

"Paine?" I throw back, relaxing just a little as he smirks at me.

"The one and only," he chuckles with a deep sexy sound. Oh yeah, now I see what Ri was trying to tell me about her wayward cousin. He's gorgeous and the shitbag knows it, I bet he has women throwing themselves at him all the time. I didn't think it could be possible but his grin widens further, twisting it from gorgeous to something that you know is hiding within its depths.

"Looks like cockiness hasn't strayed off all the family lines I see," I sass with a smile of my own.

He barks a laugh, his eyes dancing in the darkness as the overhead lights swirl in erratic patterns. The tension he was trying so hard to hide, dissipates from his body and he's relaxed as he takes a step closer to me.

"You want a drink," he asks, setting off for bar, giving me his back.

I shrug because, after this initial meeting, I am even more curious about him. He has a lot of Ri's characteristics but there is something shining within the depths of his eyes that tells me he's seen more horrors than anyone knows. I turn to face him and smile when I see him staring at me from the edge of the bar with a frown. My smirk turns into a devilish smile as I make my way over, a couple of crew members saying hi to me as I pass their table.

"What your poison?" he shouts to me, and I'm grateful this far into the club the music is even louder, which means there has to be maybe one or two speakers close by as the bass is definitely moving the floor beneath my feet.

"Jack and coke," I shout back, and he smiles wide and then leans over the bar to tell the bartender.

"The dude on the door said you were behind the bar?" I ask as I take in all the occupants of the club. There are some people I haven't seen before so they must be locals but for the most part, this place is filled with crew members.

"Yeah, I was, but then I was in the office and saw you come in on the security feed," he shrugs.

"I'm not interested if this is going where I think it is," I smile then take a mouthful of my drink.

"What do you mean?" He fakes shock and I have to laugh at how stupid he looks doing the whole innocent act. I quirk a brow at him.

"Nice try, asshole," I jibe. "You saw me on the feed, and then poof, you're standing behind me like some weirdo stalker, as I said, it is not going to happen." His eyes are as wide as saucers and I laugh harder as his innocent look morphs into a pout and that has me laughing even harder.

"I know," he laughs. "Plus I really don't fancy getting chopped up into little pieces by my cousin."

I laugh too because if he thinks Ri is the one he needs to worry about he has another thing coming because I don't need her to save my ass from anyone. My gaze is knowing and he shuffles a little which has another smirk twitching the corner of my mouth. He throws his drink back and leans over the top of the bar, pulling a black box out of nowhere.

"What's this?" I ask with a frown, and Paine smiles as he hands it to me.

"Marcus left it here for you and he asked me to give it to you if he wasn't back soon enough," he says. "Come on, open it."

Excitement bubbles in my veins as I stare at the black box with its matching black bow. The ribbon is tied so neatly I don't want to ruin it. With a deep breath, I tear into the packaging, ripping the ribbon open in one tug. The soft silk box slides open and there's something inside it in black wrapping, but the thing that catches my attention is a black piece of paper on the top. Anxiety roars to life in my veins, my head whipping up to meet Paine's gaze. He smiles at me and steps back until he's around the edge of the bar disappearing into the darkness like he wasn't here in the first place.

My eyes drop back to the paper and then back up, taking in my surroundings once more. Booths line the back wall but, for now, they're empty, I make my way to one of them. My eyes lift and drop to the box as a million questions rush through my head. I don't know what's causing this more, the fact this is the first present I've had from anyone or anxiety at what he could have written.

My ass plops onto a supple leather seat, surprise pushing back the anxiety for a second because I've made it to the seating area without seeing where I was going. Placing the box down on the table gently I lift out the note, placing it down next to the box and breaking a black wax seal over the black paper. Thank fuck it's lighter up here away from the bar area so I can see everything easier, that's how I know it's a wax seal but I can't make out the logo stamped into it.

With trembling hands I unwrap a heavy object out of the black paper, my eyes widening as a matte black handle with silver skulls sticking out of the edging comes into view. As I uncover more of the item, my eyes get wider when a knife with a black metal blade comes into my sight. What the fuck? I sit here in awe as I look at the deadly weapon, the shock has rendered me immobile. I look back over to the bar after my eyes start to itch from staring at one thing without blinking, and Paine is watching me with a smile on his face, then he winks before turning away.

Oh the sneaky little fuck, he knows what this is about! My hands shake violently and I gently place the blade in the soft fabric of the box, grabbing the note from beside it. The nerves are eating me alive as I open the thick, heavy paper, and my eyes instantly start scanning the words.

Hey Pinkie.

I know you're probably thinking what the fuck is this weirdo doing writing me a note, and yeah, you're right. But fuck it, I've never been one to be able to word things how I want to. So here it goes.

I know we said there would be no expectations or emotions or anything but I haven't been able to get you out of my fucking mind since you turned up and, baby, it's driving me crazy. It only added to the madness this morning in the shower and now I've felt you come around my cock I am never letting you go. You can fight me all you want but no matter what you do, you won't get rid of me. I know you're now probably thinking of gutting me but trust me, baby, you could kill me but I would come back and haunt your ass. Even as a ghost, you're stuck with me.

Now I best explain the blade, I went to see a friend who makes customs. I saw it and I knew I had to get it for you. It embodies everything you are.

I'll see you soon, baby, and be ready to be claimed, you can't hide from me.
Demon xx

My senses are being battered by emotions, I'm shaken that he has bought something so fucking perfect for me; I just want to melt into his arms. But then I am pissed at how he claims me like I don't have a choice in the matter. Yeah, I know some women can find that uber sexy but I'm pissed and also turned on at the same time. What the fuck?! He's gotten under my fucking skin like nobody ever has. Do I want him to stay there though?

Everything that's happened since I met him flashes to the forefront of my mind like a deliciously torturous movie. But now seeing the images, I can see things that I couldn't at the time. The way he always looked at me, even though he was losing his shit over something. The way we always seemed to gravitate to one another; the explosive chemistry. *Everything*.

The lights of the club illuminate the blade in its box, the multi-colors dancing across the black blade and it hits me. She was right; she didn't think I heard her muttering when she left the night we were talking but Ri muttered under her breath, *"You'll find your home here if you look for it."*

Dammit, she's always right. I pull my phone out of my jacket pocket and unlock the screen with my thumbprint when it rings in my hand, scaring the shit out of me. It bounces between my palms as I try to catch it, the phone still ringing; I accept the call.

"Pinkie?" Demon sounds out of breath like he's rushing somewhere. "You there?"

"I was just going to m—"

"Tell Liam I know who is causing the shit and I need his ass here now," he demands, his breathing coming heavier.

"What's happening?" I ask in a panic, I've never heard him like this before.

"Do this for me, I have so much to say to you but I can't at the moment, Pinkie, I need you to get your ass out of town and I'll f—"

"Marcus?!" I scream down the phone, but the line has already gone dead.

15

MARCUS

Shit, shit, shit!

My screen goes black as my battery dies in my hand, and my arms and legs are pumping as hard as they can to eat up the ground to get me back to my car. I should have fucking known when we got the news that someone was causing shit that it would be something to do with Pinkie's fucking dad! Our feet thud against the floor as we charge down the corridor of the warehouse. Dane's in front of me and I'm two strides behind him, taking up the rear.

"Get back here," echoes behind me, and the heavy footfalls of the group can be heard chasing us.

My lungs desperately try to suck in air as we run hard, but they are barely getting enough. My chest feels heavy and my legs are screaming in agony as we continue down another corridor. I could almost sigh in relief when I spot the doorway with the broken *Exit* sign above it. We're nearly there, the footfalls from our assailants sound further away, but that means fuck all in this moment. Dane bursts through the door, the heavy metal smacking against the wall with a massive thud, I follow a step behind and the darkness of the street comes into view. This part of town is empty this time of night, the only thing that I'm thankful for is the street lights are still on.

"Dane?" I pant as we carry on running down the street to where we left our transport.

"Yeah boss," he manages to get out, his breathing sounding like a freight train is next to me.

"Your bike's closer, I'm not sure if Ryan will find Liam. He's at The Pit, go and get him. I'll stay on the outskirts to see how many of them there are."

He nods and veers off to his bike as I run down another two blocks to my car. With a quick look over my shoulder, I expect to see the group that was chasing us to be close but there is nothing. The street stretches away from me but there's nothing, no evidence of anyone chasing us; it's silent. But that doesn't mean jack-shit. My car comes into view and I breathe my first sigh of relief, slowing my pace down to a jog. I pull the keys out of my pocket and hit the unlock button, the flash of the lights splitting the air and making me cringe at how bright it is.

Yanking the door open, I lift my leg to climb in then the world goes black.

16

RYAN

My senses are numb as I stare at the screen of my phone, the panic in his voice playing on repeat in my head. Soul-destroying fear fills me for the first time in my life and I'm frozen. I have never felt like this, the voices in my head scream at me to move my ass; that just adds to the fear because they haven't been this out of control since that night.

My vision is blurry as I try to push through the numbness keeping me in place, but no matter how much I try to break through… nothing. A shadow engulfs me and I still can't move, a heavy weight settles around my arms and I flinch for the first time in my life. Suddenly I'm shaking violently, my head like it's getting attacked inside a wave that continues to batter me and keep me under.

"Ryan!"

Everything comes back at once as Paine's terror-filled face comes into view in a pinpoint. He's standing before me with a painful grip on my arms as he pulls me forward again.

"What the fuck is going on?" he demands, dropping his hold on me.

The numbness and fear consume me for another second as

he stands there waiting for me to answer him. Then I'm off, running through the club like a mad woman, screaming at people to, "*move,*" and shoving whoever is stupid enough to ignore me. People cuss me out as I get to the door leading to the corridor before the exit.

"What's up?" Paine bellows, the sound of his voice crystal-clear for the first time, and that gives me pause as I look over to where I left him standing. My eyes widen when I notice the music is off, the lights are on, and he's barking orders at someone I can't see. Then he's striding my way.

The crew members that were lounging around are now on their feet looking between him and me.

I take off out the door, not waiting for him. My body is fueled by the command Demon gave me, it's late and there is only one place Liam has to be; The Pit. My strides eat up the ground and I run like I'm doing the hundred-meter dash, the door swinging open from the outside as two people step into the corridor, but I don't stop, plowing through them like they are not an obstacle.

The chaos from outside switches back on, and I can hear the excited chatter of the patrons waiting to get into the club, but other than that my mind is blank; Where the fuck did I leave my bike?

"Ryan?" I spin around at my name being called and a concerned Paine is looking down at me with a frown.

"Where's my bike?" I ask frantically. "I need to find my bike then get to Liam."

"Tell me what the hell has the Harbinger so fucking scared?" he demands, stepping closer to me.

"Demon needs Liam, something's happening and he rang I could tell he was running," my voice trembles and the panic builds again, my skin feeling like there are fire ants hidden under the surface. "Where's my fucking bike?!"

"You can't ride like this," he says softly, pulling me forward to tuck me into his side. "Give me your keys and I'll drive you to the Pit."

I do as I'm told, fishing the keys out of my pocket and pass them to him. He smiles down at me but I can see the surprise in his eyes, like he was expecting me to fight him on it.

"Take her bike and we'll meet you there," he says to someone, I growl in protest but then I see loads of cars and trucks screeching down the street. Lifting my eyes to meet his, I quirk a brow in question. He pulls me to his side, walking the few steps it takes to get to the curb where his truck is there idling. He holds the door open for me and I climb in, it takes only a second before he's climbing into the driver's side and the screech of tires fills the air.

"What the fuck?" I ask, bracing my hands on the dash at the way it barrels around corners feeling like it will tip over. "Who was in all those cars?"

"The crew in the club heard you say Marcus rang panicked. They followed me out because if he's scared, then the whole crew needs to worry. Especially since Reika and Kane aren't here," he answers, not taking his eyes off the road.

Shit. Ri. She's going to lose her shit if anything happens to him; she won't say it out loud but he's one of her favorite people ever. If something happens… Don't go there, he'll be fine.

Paine drives like a man possessed and we careen down street after street; The Pit comes into view and it's chaos. Cars line the road, some of them parked haphazardly like they've just been dumped. The truck brakes slam on and I jump out to the sound of Paine yelling at me in fear. But my mind is focused on the most important thing now, I yank the Pit door open and run down the corridor at full speed. My lungs are heaving and I growl at how long the fucking corridor is. I burst through the curtain and skid to a stop.

Liam's at the front of the group, in what looks like full tactical clothing, barking orders at the mass of people that makes this place look miniscule. The crowd splits up into groups and they take off with their orders, before Liam turns his attention back to the young lad I've seen around the house. I weave my way through the masses, with everyone trying to go in different directions it feels like it's taking me forever. Finally, I break through, and Liam's eyes widen when he sees me.

"Where do you want me?" I demand, lifting my chin.

"You need to get out of here, Ryan," he says softly as the guy he was just talking to walks off. "We'll go and get my brother, then he will come find you but he wants you safe."

"Fuck that!" I bellow. "I'm going with you."

"Ryan." His tone sounds exasperated.

I grit my teeth and fold my arms across my chest ready to argue with him, to everyone else I probably look like a petulant child about to throw a tantrum, but no way in hell are they leaving me out of this. It's Demon...

"I know he's your brother," I say when I notice the fear in his eyes. And I know the fear isn't because of what they're all about to walk into; no, it's for his brother, and I understand. "I know he doesn't want me there but I know first-hand what you all are walking into and I can help."

"N—"

"He's here for me," I say quietly. Liam leans forward at my words but I don't miss the wave of anger rolling off him. "I'm the reason for them being here and if anything happens to him, it will eat me alive."

"Ryan, listen to me," he says, placing a hand on each of my shoulders and bending at the waist to look into my eyes. "I know they are here for you, my brother cares a lot about you and would do whatever he has to do to keep you safe. He asked you to leave. So that's what you're going to—"

"You can't stop me!" I throw back in challenge, cutting him off.

"Paine," he growls, his arms folding across his chest as he glares at me. Arms wrap around me after the command. "Lock her ass in the office and keep her there."

My feet come off the floor as Paine hauls me towards what must be the way to the office. I roar in anger, my arms and legs flying everywhere as I try to break Paine's hold on me.

"You bastard!" I scream at Liam as he smirks, watching me being dragged away. "Paine, put me fucking down."

A grunt echoes beneath me and I smile savagely, continuing to struggle and make this as difficult as possible. It's a shame I didn't hurt him enough to let me go. Liam turns his back on me and starts following the last few stragglers near the door.

He fucking dismissed me like I was nothing. That fuels my anger and I pick up my thrashing, satisfied when I hear another grunt; then the strong hold on me disappears and I yelp as my ass hits the solid floor.

"What the fuck?!" I yell at the fucker who's glaring at me rubbing the side of his jaw.

"Fuck my life, stop screeching like a fucking banshee," he rumbles. "Before you even think about trying to run, how about you wait until they're gone, then we can follow behind?"

I rear back in shock, my eyes widening as I look at him for any indication he's lying.

"You're my cousin's childhood friend and I know what she's like; plus, I get the feeling you're worse and, honestly, I'd like to keep my balls where they are."

"No bullshit?!" I ask, pulling myself to my feet.

He shakes his head with a smirk on his face. "Let's go."

17

MARCUS

White spots dance in front of my eyes as the fucker in front of me pulls back for another swing. I can feel the blood covering my face from the gash on the side of my head and my forehead. My legs are screaming in pain as the bones are stretched towards the floor, gravity is being a bitch at the moment. But the pain isn't caused by that. This fucker has taken the bat to my left knee and I'm pretty certain my right femur is broken.

"Where is my daughter?!" the pinched-face asshole roars from behind the ugly fucker with the bat, he's swinging it in a circle like he's winding himself up for another blow; like the good little dog he is waiting for his master's command.

The voices are screaming at me to end these bastards where they stand. It doesn't matter to the voices that I'm chained like an animal carcass hanging from the ceiling. I wouldn't be able to stand up at this point though.

I have to give her dad and his crew their dues though; they know how to play. I start to chuckle at Pinkie's dad getting redder in the face from my silence. I know it's him. It was obvious when I woke up how quickly the others jumped to his orders. Am I impressed by him? Not a fucking bit, he reminds me of a wealthier version of my father and he was a primo dick too.

"What are you laughing at, boy?" he demands, getting closer to me, the one with the bat only a step behind.

"I'm wondering, do you measure your dicks regularly to make sure you're still the top dog?" I ask with a smirk. "Because it seems to me your dog here is the only one that seems to have the balls to do anything."

"Where is my daughter?!" he screams, getting up in my face, then my smirk twists into a grin and I throw my head forward, connecting with his nose.

He squeals like a girl as his nose explodes and he falls on his ass, the others in the warehouse watching on with wide eyes. The ugly fucker rushes to pick his boss up off the floor that's cussing up a shit storm. But it stops as soon as my laughter echoes around the room, all eyes turning to me.

"I don't have a clue who your daughter is." *Lie*. "But if I had seen her around, seeing this shit, I don't blame her for getting as far away from you as possible."

My head whips back and pain explodes around my eye socket, my vision failing me as darkness tries to consume me. I manage to fight it back, my vision clearing enough to see her dad rubbing at his knuckle with his top lip curled up in disgust.

"Did you just backhand me like a little bitch?" I laugh as he lunges for me again. "Well if you ever put your hands on her like that, I one thousand percent don't blame her."

The ugly fucker whispers something to the other one and I so wish I could hear what they're arguing about. There's a problem with that though, I can feel my strength waning the longer I try to keep myself conscious.

"Where's the Reaper?!" he demands, his hands stuffed into

the pocket of his grey slacks. "She and my daughter are friends. She'll know where she is."

"Holiday," I fire back with another smile.

The ugly fucker swings again, and blood flies out of my mouth as a fire rips through my ribs on my left side. The force of the blow swings my body side to side and the bastard looks at me in triumph.

"Your spunk is admirable, boy," he says, taking a step to me. "Just tell me where she is and I'll let you live."

"Kill me," I roar, losing myself to the anger that's burning like an inferno. "I'll die before telling you shit!"

I spit blood at him, cackling when he jumps back away from it like my blood is poison. The bat clatters to the floor, then the ugly fucker pulls out a gun from the holster that was tucked under his armpit. He strides forward, pushing the barrel into my mouth; a stoic look on his face as his owner steps up behind him.

"Is that your final answer?" he drawls, the tone bored.

I narrow my eyes on him, telling them to 'Do it' but it comes out muffled by the barrel, the words not able to form properly. The smirk he gives me is cold, and I don't look away but I throw up a promise to the night that I will willingly go if my family make sure she's happy. It took me too fucking long to realize what I felt about Ryan Davenport but now that my time is over, I really wish I had told her I love her.

I love her to the bottom of my blackened being.

I never thought I'd have what my brother does but she snuck under my skin without me even knowing, implanted herself there like a brand throughout my body. I breathe out a content sight as I hear the hammer pull back, happy knowing she going to be safe.

Bang.

EPILOGUE
RYAN

"I can't do this," I mutter as I head to the door, my body heavy at the weight of everything feeling like it's crushing me.

"Don't you dare fucking leave," Ri's words cut through the silent room like a whip crack, and hearing the anger in her voice directed at me makes me feel even worse.

My feet freeze when I hear her stride towards me, a growl in her throat. I see Liam sitting in the corner of the room. He's the furthest he can be from everyone, but his face is stricken with anguish. He lifts his eyes to look at me, and I break the connection. I can't look at any of them as the guilt eats me.

"Ryan, if you try to leave once more, I swear to everything I will beat you within an inch of your life," Reika growls from my back.

"If she wants to go, let her," Kane snarls from deeper within the room, I don't know if he's still sitting in the seats he and Reika were occupying a moment ago.

"He's right," I say as my hand grabs the handle.

"She saved your brother's fucking life, you ungrateful

twat!" she screams at her other half, the pain and anger mixing together, making a deadly sound. "She got there in time."

"He's right," I say defeated. "I got lucky, but, Ri, if I had been a second later."

A sob escapes at the thought of me being a split second too late. My legs give way beneath me and the emotions become too much. Memories of earlier batter the front of my mind, as do the ones from when my mother died and I found out.

"He made it through the surgery, Ry," Ri says, kneeling on the floor in front of me. "Do you really think leaving would do you both any good?" she asks and I nod, I'm the reason we're waiting for him to wake up, why he had to have OFRI surgery.

"He's better off without me," I say harshly, wiping the tears off my cheeks. "They don't call me Harbinger for no reason."

The screech of chairs has us both glancing up as the doctor walks into the room looking tired. Ri drags me to my feet, then practically yanks me to the front of the group who are all glaring at the poor doctor.

"He's asking for you," he says, his eyes fixed on me.

"No, he will ask for one of these." My chest crumbles a little further as the doctor looks confused.

"You're Ryan?" he asks. I nod my head, even though my eyes dart either side of me. "Follow me."

Ri shoves me forward and I nearly fall flat on my face behind the doctor, but I manage to get my footing before that happens. I look over my shoulder and she smiles at me, but the look of relief on her face cuts me deep. I am only a step behind the doctor as we walk down the short hallway. He stands at the side of a door that's already open and I feel my steps start to slow.

"He's been awake for a while but he wouldn't let us tell anyone until he was ready," he says before walking off.

I tug at the tips of my fingernails, standing at the threshold of the door, and the sight that I see has me wanting to run as fast as I can away from here. He looks so weak, he's covered in bandages and dressings from the copious amounts of injuries and I don't know what that is that's keeping his knee in place. My stomach rolls as the doctor's words from when we brought him in spring to the front of my mind.

"*He's badly injured, not just from all the cuts he has. He also has a broken kneecap, but the thing we're more concerned about is his broken right femur. He needs to have surgery straight away to fix it.*"

"Don't just stand there, Pinkie."

My feet grow roots into the floor at how low his voice is, I can hear the strain. Our eyes connect and everything lifts. I rush over to him, dropping down into the chair at the side of his bed as I grab hold of his hand.

"I'm so sorry," I sob, leaning forward. "I wouldn't normally show my emotions like this to anyone but I'm just so happy he's here. "I never meant for anyone to get hurt, I should have stuck to my guns and left a couple of days earlier."

"Don't do that," he growls, but it comes out as more of a croak than anything else. "You're not to blame for this. Your crazy ass dad is," he says then goes pensive for a moment. "What happened?"

"I got to you just in time, Liam ordered Paine to lock me in the office, but he didn't want to lose his balls so we left just after the others," I say, biting my lip. "My gut told me to go to the warehouse where we… you know. I got sight of you just as my father's second pulled back the hammer."

"How am I still here? I heard the shot fire?" he asks confused.

"The shot was mine," I say, sitting up to meet his eyes. "When I saw you there with the barrel in your mouth I reacted, I killed him. I was about to take another shot at my father, but

Liam chose that moment to burst through the door with the crew so me and Paine got you to the hospital."

"Thank you," he says, his eyes shining with emotion; I'm not sure which one.

He pulls me forward, his lips fusing to mine as he kisses me with a softness I never knew he could have. My heart rate picks up as our kiss deepens, making me lightheaded when he pulls back with a smile on his face.

"I meant everything in that letter, now I've had you, Pinkie; I am not letting you go." His tone is determined as he watches me. "You got a problem with that?"

"You're stuck with me too, Demon, so let's cause some chaos together."

The End...

AFTERWORD

How are you all feeling? I know Marcus and Ryan's story is a lot shorter than Book 1 but honestly, I think it just fits for who they both are as people. The Damned Crew was originally only meant to be the first couple's story but as the other characters progressed, I soon realized I wanted to give them their own happily ever afters. Marcus has just had his but make sure you're following along on all socials to keep up to date as the other boys and someone else will be getting their own stories.

I hope you enjoyed Marcus and Ryan as much as I did and I'm glad Cheshire got to get his happily ever. Even the darkest soul deserves love and to find someone who accepts them just as they are.

ACKNOWLEDGMENTS

I want to say a huge thank you to my daughters and my family for your ongoing support and for putting up with me missing family events. My girls are the world to me and the driving force behind everything I do, the seriously early mornings and the long hours of writing. I love you both to the moon and back.

My amazing Alpha team, your ladies are life; honestly, without you all putting up with my squirrelly butt I don't know what I would do. You're there when I throw stuff at you all last minute or when I go radio silent for weeks at a time. You ladies are the best so thank you so much.

My beta team, you ladies are amazing too and I can't you all enough for coming on board and becoming my team.

I want to say a massive thank you to everyone at Hudson Indie Ink for everything you do and the wealth of knowledge you all have. Claire Boyle, you are the most amazing person ever and I'm going to say sorry now for the headaches I know I've more than likely caused.

To Lily Bennett you missy are awesome, the way you bring books to life with formatting just blows my mind every time, and you are awesome, you're one of my favorite people.

Sarah Goodman, you're the most amazing person ever. The help and guidance you have given me is something I am so grateful for I can't even explain how glad I am to know you as a person and to call you my friend.

ABOUT THE AUTHOR

Tatum Rayne was born in a small town in West Yorkshire. From a young age she has always had a wild imagination and had to put pen to paper, after deciding to finally chase her dream her debut Ruthless Monsters was released in 2022. She still lives in her hometown with her own family, which is the driving force behind her. When she isn't writing, or having spontaneous days out. She loves to curl up with a coffee and a book or have a Netflix binge. Tatum writes deliciously Dark contemporary and PNR romances from Academy Bully to Mafia while enjoying mixing it up between MF and Whychoose. That will leave you in hot sweats while putting your emotions on a rollercoaster of a journey that will leave you wanting to devour it all.

To keep up to date on everything you can follow along on social media or even sign up for my newsletter to get the first look at all upcoming releases, cover reveals and so much more, join my newsletter!

ALSO BY TATUM RAYNE

MORGANSYTH ACADEMY

(Rejected Mates, Academy MF Romance)

Poison

BROAD CREEK PREP

(Dark, Academy, MF Romance)

Broken Prince

BLACK FROST ACADEMY DUET

(Dark, Bully, College-age Academy, Why choose Romance)

Black Frost Academy

Return to Black Frost Academy

THE DAMNED CREW

(Dark, Mafia MF Romance)

Ruthless Monsters

OTHER AUTHORS AT HUDSON INDIE INK

Paranormal Romance/Urban Fantasy

Stephanie Hudson

Xen Randell

C. L. Monaghan

Sorcha Dawn

Harper Phoenix

Crime/Action

Blake Hudson

Jack Walker

Contemporary Romance

Gemma Weir

Nikki Ashton

Anna Bloom

Tatum Rayne

Milton Keynes UK
Ingram Content Group UK Ltd.
UKHW022134280224
438615UK00001B/5